ONE BAD WISH

BONNIE ELIZABETH

My Big Fat Orange Cat Publishing

One Bad Wish
My Big Fat Orange Cat
Contemporary Fantasy, May 2017

My Big Fat Orange Cat Publishing
MyBigFatOrangeCat.com

Chapter One

"You can't control the wish"

— from the Fairy Godmother's Handbook

Being a fairy godmother isn't something I ever intended to become. I mean, I wasn't born that way —now that's a scary thought, me in a fairy dress and sparkles all over me as a baby. Yuck. No, I wished the fairy godmother gig into being kind of by accident, and I've been stuck granting wishes for the last six months or so.

It's not all bad. Basically, I'd been lucky—or unlucky, depending upon your point of view—to have made the wish that started it all. In a nutshell, I met this creepazoid old guy at the Farmer's Market who told me to make a wish. So I stupidly wished to make people happy, meaning someone, anyone, because although I had done exactly what I had told my mother I said I would do, she was still not happy. And *wham*. There I was. A Fairy Godmother. There's more, of course, but that's a whole other story.

Being able to grant wishes is kind of cool. About once a week, sometimes more, sometimes less, I get this urge, like a pressure and I have to go out and find someone wishing for something. It's not that hard. I can think about a place that draws people to make wishes, you know, like wishing wells and crap like that, or I can just think myself over to someone wishing. Then I grant the wish.

I don't get a lot of choice in how it happens. I mean, I grant a lot of cute kittens to cute kids and stuff. I've wanted to grant a zombie cat instead, but the magic doesn't work that way. Probably a good thing, because I'm not really sure what would happen to the world if I was able to grant zombie kittens.

But yeah, that's how I think. Even so, I'm not sure I'd really do something like that, but it's kind of cool to think about the implications and everything, ya know? I mean, cute kid wants cat and I send them a re-animated creature straight out of the LOLcat version of the Walking Dead?

Unfortunately I don't get to talk to people about this much. It's a secret that I'm a fairy godmother. Although, would you really go around saying, "Hey, yeah, I'm a fairy godmother now!" Cause that's just weird. Besides, I'd get everyone wanting me to grant their wishes.

It's bad enough that I can always hear sentences that start with "I wish". In high school, at least *my* high school, people are always saying "I wish this" or "I wish that." Really, really annoying when you're someone who hears about wishes. Fortunately, I can't grant them all, largely because I don't want to, not to mention that most of the things people say aren't real wishes, even if they do start with "I wish." But even if I could, there are rules. I'm not even sure what all the rules are. There's this huge book of rules that I got when I became a fairy godmother—a file just appeared on my computer, can you believe it?—but besides being major league style boring it's pretty vague about a ton of stuff. Come to think of it, there's probably something in there about why I can't grant zombie kittens, but I'm not going to go digging for it.

Last night, I think I granted a wish I shouldn't have or something. Remember what I said about zombie kittens? I don't get a choice. If you're there wishing and I'm there with wish-granting power, well *Kabam!* The wish is yours. No matter what. Even if it's a bad wish.

I've granted a few bad wishes. Mostly those are only a problem for the person who made the wish. Like this girl wished to never gain weight and now she's in the hospital. See, she got sick and lost a bunch of weight and now she can't gain it back. Still in the hospital because, you know, too thin. So yeah, there are problems with wishes. I didn't get a good feeling granting that wish and mostly I do, even cliché, stupid, puppies-and-kittens-for-kids wishes. It's embarrassing to have to say that, so don't tell.

This wish, the one I can't remember and think I probably shouldn't have granted? Well, I was wiped out. So wiped out that I just went to bed right after and couldn't really remember what I had done. I knew I'd granted a wish, but I couldn't remember it, which was different. Not just different, but like *really* different. And this morning I ached all over like I had the flu.

Still, it was Friday and I didn't want to take a sick day when everyone else was likely to be goofing off anyway, so I got myself up. I pretty much noticed things weren't quite right but they weren't all that wrong, either.

My phone alarm was on a different ring, pretty annoying. My bedroom had lavender and black stripes instead of *purple* and black stripes. That kind of gave me a scare, but my stuff was all where it should be…mostly.

It was less like I was in the wrong place than that someone had shared the house with me or something. I couldn't exactly remember what was wrong but there were things like the colors in my room that weren't right. My bed was in the right place, along the wall the window was in, and the dresser was still right beside it. The desk was still the same light wood as the dresser and still sat kind of at the foot of the bed. Normal, right?

I didn't smell eggs and bacon downstairs. Instead, I smelled something that was suspiciously like those toaster tart things that I sneaked over at my friend Sage's house. My mom is like totally into healthy food that she makes mostly from scratch. Toaster tarts are so *not* on the menu at our house.

Yes, in my mom's world, bacon is healthy. We get it from a pig that lived in luxury, next door, and was prayed over for three days before being slaughtered, and the bacon that comes out is made from only the purest of the pure by unicorns dancing in the sun. Okay. Not really. But you get the idea that my mom is into local, organic, and humanely-raised food. She's like this cross between the big time food police and a total crunchy hippy-dippy, woo-woo lady. The first time I heard the phrase "yogurt and granola," I totally knew it described my mom exactly.

Anyway, I dressed. It was going to be a pretty nice day, so I wore my favorite jeans in stonewashed blue and a navy tank top under a yellow t-shirt. That should be enough. I combed through my hair and went downstairs.

My brother wasn't there yet. He's always the first to breakfast and the first out the door. It's not like I care. I mean he's older and everything and kind of does his own thing. Boys know me because he'd bring them by and I was always trying to hang out with them. When I was little, it was sort of like because I liked my brother and wanted to do the same things he did. He hated that. Now, he gets a kick out of reminding me. Like thanks.

Anyway, Mom was there, with a newspaper, in a nice pair of slacks eating a toaster tart. And I'm all, "What's that?"

"What's what?" she asked absently.

"What you're eating?"

"Willow?" She looked up at me. She was clearly confused.

I looked in the fridge. It was full of store-bought ketchup and mustard and even salad dressing in a bottle, but not one of the recycled bottles that mom usually puts the homemade stuff into. There was salad in one of those plastic boxes and non-organic deli meat. I didn't even have to push aside the organic and locally grown fruits and vegetables to find what I was looking for.

Fortunately there was yogurt, but it wasn't organic and definitely not the plain stuff where I had to mix my own berries and crap into it. I grabbed a convenience yogurt, wondering if I was making a mistake. Normally, toaster tarts are a treat, and I'd go for those, but I didn't feel that great and yogurt seemed like it would be easier on my stomach.

"Where's Eric?" I asked.

"He's got five minutes before he has to be out the door. I'm sure he'll be down," my mother said calmly.

Okay, so that was big clue that something was majorly wrong. It went beyond the food and the actions. It was like my mom's whole attitude. She didn't even seem worried, and my mom loves to worry about things while telling the rest of the world not to worry. Probably because she's doing all of it for them. It kind of made my stomach feel all lumpy and funny which totally did not put me in a good mood for the morning.

Still, I finished up my yogurt, hardly tasting the overly-sweet blueberry flavoring. I was a little disappointed that there wasn't more in the cup. I'm used to filling a bowl with the plain stuff and adding a bunch of berries and homemade granola. This was just not enough, but I wasn't going to whine too much, at least not then. Things were weird enough. What if I was in some alternate universe and my mom got suspicious that I wasn't really me and locked me up?

Okay, maybe I have a bit of a wild imagination, but I'm a freaking fairy godmother, so I think I'm entitled. I try to use my imagination for good, which is usually adding snarky comments to whatever the day's trending topic is.

I left the house, carrying my backpack, hoping that I'd been organized enough to put everything I might need in there the night before. I wasn't sure what I actually needed —I mean, I knew what I needed in the world I'd been in when I fell asleep but this didn't appear to be that world. It was too early for me to have an idea of what world it was, but I had a niggling suspicion it had to do with the wish I granted the day before.

Of course, I had to wonder too, was I still dreaming? I pinched myself, which hurt, but nothing changed, outside of the fact that now my arm was sore. I tried to get myself to open my eyes, but nothing changed. And you know how it feels different to be in a dream rather than in the real world? This *felt* real.

Now, you might be thinking that I'm taking all this in stride and you'd be both right and wrong. I mean, it *seemed* like it was my world. The yard looked the same, if a little less perfectly kept. There were way fewer weeds, but the lines between the flower garden and the yard weren't as neat. There was also a plain, ordinary tree with pink flowers that we didn't have in our real yard. In our *real* yard we had a cherry tree that flowered, but it also had fruit, so in case of the zombie apocalypse and we had to live off our little less than a quarter of an acre of suburban land, we had a chance of doing so, I guess, although I doubt that we'd be able to live off of what we grew now.

Still, the tree thing got me. I hurried across the street. I saw the yellow of the bus coming down and heard the squeal of breaks as it stopped at the stop sign a block away.

Sage came out of her front door. She looked thinner than she was in my world, but maybe I was looking for things. Her face was also harder, like she'd spent the last two years being angry about things rather than laughing, you know? Eric came flying out the door just as the bus pulled up, and he ran around behind it while the rest of us got on.

"You were early," Sage said when we sat down behind a Goth-looking girl. It took me a minute to realize that the girl with the super black hair and pale skin was actually my friend Ashley. I had an internal shiver and thought I remembered granting a wish for her. I couldn't remember the wish. Another odd thing to add to the day of odd things.

I watched the other kids getting in. Tenisha sat with Dulce and the two of them didn't turn or look at anyone else, which was kinda normal. Tenisha's hair was braided in thicker braids than it normally was, and it looked like she might have a little bit of a reddish tint. She and Ash were good friends—in my world—so it was a surprise that Ashley hadn't said anything to her.

My brother was in the back of the bus with the usual crowd of guys he sat with. Sometimes he'd get a ride with Doug Layton when Doug got the car, but mostly he rode the bus. This was all normal-but-not-quite-normal. Like the world had tipped just a little bit.

"Just not feeling quite right," I said, slowly. Sage was sitting next to the window and I had the aisle seat. The seat felt harder than our usual seat but, again, like Sage looking thinner and harder, it could have been my imagination. Maybe it wasn't. Maybe going to school wasn't such a good idea. I wondered how I could get a hold of the other fairy godmothers. It's not like we have a 911 number to call in case of an emergency.

That's right, there are a bunch of us. We meet every Monday night at seven in the junkiest place around, but there are issues with changing that so we don't. You would think, though, that a group of people who can grant wishes could find a place better than a leaky basement that never gets warm, with a bunch of mismatched, broken-down furniture. But maybe that's just me.

At any rate, I had a feeling Monday was going to be too far away, so I needed to figure out a way to contact someone right now. The handbook of rules and things was on my computer at home. Maybe I could get sick about halfway through and go home? Or something?

"I'd of stayed home," Sage said. She turned away from me and looked out the window. She had a large hickey on her neck, towards the back that I hadn't noticed before. In my world, Sage didn't have a steady boyfriend, although she was interested in Doug Layton, the quarterback. He and Eric hung out a lot, and I knew Doug way too well to be interested in him. I couldn't believe Sage was.

"Thought about it," I said. "But I didn't want my mom to get all freaked out."

"Like your mom freaks about anything," Sage laughed. There was something harsh there. Besides, Sage knew better. My mom freaked about *everything*, certain I was ingesting toxins by merely existing. But the mom who sat unconcerned reading the newspaper this morning in a nice set of clothes and not pants that looked homemade, well she didn't seem worried about anything. Sage could be right.

I shrugged. "No sense in starting on a weekend." That sounded like me, I hoped. But maybe I was a different person in this world?

Sage laughed again, that harsh bark of a laugh that was completely unlike her.

The bus turned into the school drop off area, finally, and I stood up, probably too quickly. Sage gave me a look, surprised and not at all pleased but she followed me out. Ashley, the Goth girl, sat and watched us, her eyes narrowed. I tried to smile, but she only glared.

"What was that?" Sage asked as I jumped off the last step.

"What?" Outside the school looked mostly the same. There were still five low steps in a semi-circle leading up to the main doors. There was a large overhang that kept people dry and cool when they had to wait to go through the metal detectors. There was the same smell of bleach and coffee that permeated the air near the building. Inside, I had no doubt the scent of dirty socks was still part of the mix.

It was still a long low building that looked smaller than what it was on the inside. The roof was still blue, although I thought it was a darker blue, like it had been painted more recently than the one in my world. The cream colored siding along the walls and the windows mostly looked the same, although some of the window decorations looked a little different, but not so much as I'd have noticed if I wasn't looking for it.

"Talking to Goth girl?" Sage said like it was the worst thing in the world.

Now, normally Sage and I hung with Ashley and Lauren. Lauren made a big deal out of the new, "nicer," me because I no longer snarked about everything. It's hard to do when you grant wishes, but I did my best. Ashley was almost as bad. The fact that we weren't friends in this world was troubling, and it made my stomach hurt worse. Not that we were that good of friends that I'd be worried about that in general. I had a feeling it had to do with a wish—probably one Ashley made.

Did she hate me so much that she'd wished we weren't friends? I couldn't believe that would change so many things. There was something even more wrong.

I walked up the steps with Sage, not answering her, thinking about *how* to answer. Maybe not saying anything was better than defending myself. I got through the metal detector without setting anything off. I was glad to see Brad, the regular security guard there and looking like an older, worn version of a cartoon genie, with his bald head and heavy arms.

He greeted me the way Brad always did, which was exactly like he greeted all the other kids. At least someone was exactly the same. Did that mean whatever Ashley wished hadn't really affected him? Which was interesting. I mean, would it affect the entire school or just the people close to her? I wished I remembered what her wish was. It might help me make sense of this.

I grabbed my bag and headed down the hall to my homeroom. There were the usual bulletin boards on the left and lockers on the right side of the hallway. I turned right, with Sage following right behind me, not saying anything. I paused to let her catch up. She turned to give me a look and passed by without a word. Now that was weird. At any rate, I followed her into our homeroom.

The seats were arranged the same way, at least as far as I could tell. I sat towards the back with Sage. She didn't seem to notice that I was sitting there, so that meant I must be in the right seat. A few people gave me waves. Sage started talking to Lauren the moment she walked in. Both of them sort of ignored me. I wondered if this was part of my role in this world or if I'd done something to piss Sage off.

Sage tends to clam up when she's pissed off. Of course, normally she eventually does talk to me and she doesn't usually give me the cold shoulder unless I'm well aware of why. This time I had no idea what was going on. Which meant I'd done something wrong. I had no idea if my problem had started that morning or earlier. It wasn't like I understood this world. I tried not to sulk.

The whole my-world/this-world thing was frustrating. I mean yesterday things were normal and the way I knew them. This post-wish fantasy world was really irritating. I needed to have a way to clarify things for myself and for any other fairy godmothers I had to tell about this. "The real world", or maybe "pre-wish world", and "post-wish world" seemed like good ways of labeling them.

Mrs. Charpentier called roll as she always did, using our full names. As usual I wiggled my pen at her and she nodded, although there was the slightest raise of an eyebrow. Okay, so I must speak or something here. But how would I know those things? Maybe I ought to tell her I just didn't feel good. Sage would likely back me up, *if* she wasn't mad enough at me for not acting right that she was completely ignoring me.

I listened to the announcements. Then we moved onto our English lesson and the reading. It was the same lesson

I'd done for Wednesday in my world, which made things a little easier. But while that was sort of a relief, it also worried me. What if I got to a class where I had to know things I wasn't supposed to study for another few days in the real world? Or worse, what if things like history were different in this world?

I almost started to hyperventilate thinking about that, but calmed myself by focusing on the words in front of me. It was just a few hours. I could get through this.

"I so wish this class would end," I heard the voice of Mr. Tremayne in the other room. He was my math teacher. I was used to hearing that wish from him. He hated the first period students. They were his most difficult class, and I kind of had to laugh because that was the class he was always certain was never going to end. He didn't need to wish for it to end, because that would happen whether he wished it or not.

Now that I'd clearly granted a wish or something that was bad, I had to wonder what would happen if he ever said those words when I was ready to grant a wish. Would we all just lose an hour of time? Or would something worse happen?

Chapter Two

"Anyone can become a fairy godmother,
regardless of who they are."

— *from the Fairy Godmother's Handbook*

I acted like a zombie through English and math. History was third period, and I hoped that most of history was still the same. So far I'd been doing okay. Sage was in a different math class and a different history class, just like in our real life. Lauren was in my history class, which was an honors level, but unlike in my real, pre-wish life, she didn't sit next to me.

I looked around the room when I walked in. Everything on the walls, the maps and the articles looked the same on first glance. That meant any changes probably weren't so big that I couldn't fake my way through things. At least I could hope.

Ashley was in that class, but ignored me completely. In

fact, it appeared that Ashley, who was one of the most popular girls in my pre-wish school, had no friends at all in this post-wish world. She sat by herself in the back. She didn't talk to anyone. She ignored the teacher, giving only the briefest of signals as he called roll. I watched from the corner of my eye. No way was I going to be caught looking directly at her. Who knows what I'd get myself into if I did?

Lauren sat a few rows over and glared at Ashley several times but I couldn't discern a reason. I was sitting next to Cherize, a heavy-set girl—okay a fat girl—that I know slightly in my pre-wish world. She was still fat, but she was outgoing and nice and she talked a blue streak at me. Not something she normally would have done in my world. But it felt good. Someone saw me and talked to me.

"I'm just not feeling my best," I said. It was the sort of thing my mother would have said and it really did describe how I felt. I shifted a little in the narrow classroom seat, trying to put more space between me and the desk. I'd have liked to lie down and think, but that wasn't going to happen. Had the seats at my school been this hard and this small? And when did the history room smell vaguely like rotten eggs?

"Then maybe you need to go to the nurse," Cherize said. "I can't believe Sage didn't like announce it or something in English."

I tried to think back. Yep, Cherize was in English but she sat on the other side of the room. Sage wasn't the sort to announce things at any time, but I let that comment pass. After all, this Sage wasn't exactly the Sage who was my best friend.

"Well I wasn't that bad then, so maybe she thought it would pass." I smiled to lighten that up.

Cherize didn't look convinced. "I don't know why you stay friends with her. She's so mean to you."

"We've been friends forever," I protested. Sage and I had grown up across the street from each other. Our mothers were friends, bonding over some adult thing or other. Sage and I were thrown together when we were little, and our friendship was sort of forced into being. It bothered me that I couldn't remember why they were such close friends.

Sage's mom worked at the dental office around the corner where we both had our teeth cleaned and stuff like that. My mom, of course, didn't work outside the home. She was too busy making homemade clothes and all natural food. She often gave extras to Sage's family. In the late summer there was usually a canning party.

I pictured Mom's last canning party. Our dads were outside with the giant black barbeque and talking about the best way to light a fire, because I guess that's the sort of thing men talked about. They were out there a long time so either it's really interesting to dads or they found something else to discuss.

Sage and I had gone up to the television room to watch a movie before my brother came in and ruined that for us. We'd then moved out to the sun. Fortunately by that time the barbeque discussion was over and Sage and I could relax in the zero-gravity chairs my folks had scattered around the patio. I got the blue and white one. Sage got the slightly newer red and white one.

I couldn't remember if Ashley and Lauren had come last year or the year before. Sometimes they came with their moms, who always had to watch my mother do the canning. Once, Ashley's younger brother had come, but my brother... my memory trailed off. Ashely didn't have a brother did she? I tried to picture him but I couldn't. Still, there was something very clear about the fact that my brother did something to her brother and it wasn't nice. I tried to remember. Maybe my brother had called him an annoying baby? That sounded right in my head, but it was vague, like a dream.

"What if Ashley had a brother?" I asked Cherize.

"What if? You think she'd be more popular?" Cherize asked. "I suppose if he were older and really good-looking and everyone wanted to get to know him."

Well that answered that question. In this post-wish world, Ashley didn't have a brother. I was equally certain that in my world, the real, pre-wish world, she did. Had she wished her brother out of existence? My stomach clenched like I was going to toss.

I must have looked as bad as I felt.

"Mr. Harrison?" Cherize was standing up and waving her hand. "Can I take Willow to the nurse? I think she's going to be sick."

Mr. Harrison looked up from the board he was writing on.

"I trust this isn't just your opinion of the work today?" he asked drily.

I shook my head. I really needed to lie down or something. Maybe actually vomit or just curl up in a ball. This felt a little like the need to grant a wish but it had an emptiness that I hadn't felt before.

Mr. Harrison felt around in his desk, keeping an eye on the rest of us and pulled out a hall pass. Cherize helped me out of my seat. She packed away my books and put my backpack on her shoulder. She left her things. The class hadn't really even started and no doubt she'd be back before Mr. Harrison even finished writing on the board, assuming this class was like the class he ran in the pre-wish world.

"Thanks," I said as we got out the door.

"Hey, it's worth it to miss a little of class. Too bad you don't look like you're faking. We could have had some fun."

I grinned at her. Maybe I needed to get to know this girl a little better. She certainly seemed nicer than the Sage of this world. Maybe I was a nicer person, too, not that I really felt a need to be nicer. I was who I was. And I was already getting a bit sappy, what with granting kitten-and-puppy-wishes to little kids.

Anyway, the hallway was quiet. I rarely walked the halls while classes were in session, so I had no idea if this were normal or not. Mrs. Phish was in the principal's office and she had me sit down while she called the nurse. Cherize was told to give me my backpack and get back to class. Mrs. Phish made a quick note on her hall pass and then Cherize waved a few fingers at me while she left.

There was a window behind the ordinary metal chair that I sat in. Fortunately the chair had a bit of padding although not nearly enough. I turned to watch Cherize walk back down the wide hall. She was clearly taking her time. The clock on the wall over Mrs. Phish's desk, ticked twice before the receptionist returned.

Mr. Buchowski, the school nurse and football coach, came out from his office that sat near the principal's office.

"So you're sick?" he asked, standing in front of me so that if I looked at him directly I'd see his crotch, which is not something you want to see on a guy who could play football. He reminded me a lot of Brian, one of the fairy godmothers. Brian also reminded me of a football player. Unlike Mr. Buchowski, Brian had never played football, nor was he interested in doing so. Yeah, I know. Brian is probably not what you picture when you think fairy godmother.

I kept my head down and nodded at him.

Buchowski helped me stand up and walked me towards his office. This office had a lot of windows into the main office, where Mrs. Phish and anyone else in the office could see in. I suppose that was to make the kids feel safe, so they weren't alone with a guy like Buchowski, as if Mrs. Phish could take him on if he did do any messing around. Of course, even feeling like dog crap, I'd be kicking Buchowski in the nuts and running if he tried something with *me*.

I sat on the sofa that was under the outside window. Mrs. Phish was back at her desk, pointedly not looking at us.

Buchowski pulled out a digital thermometer and stuck it in my ear to take my temperature. It beeped in no time. I smelled the faint scent of disinfectant as he pulled it out and that messed up the coffee and gym socks odor the permeated the office. Now I remembered why I wasn't thrilled about being at the nurse's office.

"Only slightly high," Buchowski said. "What's going on?"

"I feel really crampy," I said. It was an honest answer. That way I could curl up on my side and groan if I needed to. Maybe I'd have to grant a wish and someone would wish away the wish I had inadvertently granted.

I couldn't have said anything better. Buchowski turned a bright red and then stammered. He was on the phone in no time, probably to my mom, to tell her daughter was sick with female problems. Who knew that would work so well?

I held my stomach and groaned a little for effect. Cherize would be proud. Oh hell, in my world, Sage and Lauren would have laughed themselves silly. Even Ashley would have been impressed.

Chapter Three

Memory loss on the part of the granter means they inadvertently granted a wish that should never have been granted

—from the Fairy Godmother's Handbook

My mom was not pleased when she got to school to pick me up. She was dressed in those nice pants, pants I'd never seen her wear before, and a red top that looked like something off the rack. I was sure it was polyester, which was like the biggest no-no since high fructose corn syrup. It was a nice color on her though, which wasn't something she normally worried about.

My pre-wish mom probably would have started singing to me to. Whenever something bad happened she was always starting to sing that Disney movie song, *"A Whole New World."* The problem is, my mom has a horrible voice and she can't reach the high notes nor can she sustain the notes at all. It's a major joke at our house. This post-wish mom was not singing—nor did she look like she was plan-ning to break out in any song.

"You weren't sick when you were home?" my mom said, in a voice that sounded more accusing than worried.

"Not really. I thought I was just tired but then I got all crampy and my head felt weird." Both of those things were true enough. I did feel kind of crampy. And my head did feel weird although it was mostly weird because things were not normal in Willow's world. Let's just say *confused* would have been a perfectly acceptable way of describing what was going on in my head, but I doubted post-wish Mom would have allowed such a thing.

"So instead you tried to tough it out, without thinking that I might have to leave work to come get you?" Mom sounded really upset.

I really wanted to ask where she worked but I suspected that wouldn't go over well. At least I could probably count on the fact that this mom would go rushing back to work while I stayed home and checked things out on my computer, like my rule book.

"I really did think it would pass," I said. "I didn't think it would get worse."

She nodded shortly and didn't say much else. She led me outside to a gray SUV that wasn't even a hybrid. My pre-wish mom would have had a major snit-fit about this car. First, it was brand-spanking new. It even had that new car smell inside when I got in. It also had to use way more gasoline than it needed to. What had happened to her?

I climbed in and fastened my seatbelt, looking around at all the gadgets.

"If you're well enough to oogle the car again, Willow, are you sure you can't stay in school?" Mom asked. There was an edge to her voice that I was familiar with, although not usually in this situation.

"It's fun to oogle. Besides that doesn't take any thinking." I turned my head and looked out at the school. It looked so mostly-normal but underneath it wasn't at all. Yes, the outside looked the same, the same curving steps, the same awning, the same scuffed-gray metal detectors. But inside, the people. They were different. Even the pre-wish Mrs. Phish would have recognized me and spoken to me when I was in the nurse's office instead of just going on about her work

I wanted to cry a little, partly because I felt really lousy, but also because if I had to feel lousy, I wanted my mom to be someone I knew. What if I was stuck in this post-wish world forever? I mean would I have to relearn history? How would I know who my friends were? What if I didn't even like my friends?

The drive took forever. One thing that hadn't changed was that Mom was a super cautious driver. Which meant that even school buses, making all the usual stops, would have beaten her to the house. I tried to bite back any sighs. I didn't want any more attention than I'd had. I mean, it was stressful enough trying to fit in, but trying to fit into a world that you didn't really know was even worse.

"I'm dropping you here," Mom said, not getting out of the car. "Because you look like you can make it inside. I'll call at lunch to see if you need anything. But don't expect me to drop everything again to help out for anything short of an actual emergency."

"I'm sure I'll be okay. I think I just need some more sleep," I said, dropping out of the car. I pulled my backpack with me.

"See that you get some. No watching movies all afternoon!" My mom put the car in reverse before I even slammed the door, which I did a little harder than I should have, but fortunately it was a big car and she didn't notice.

She was backing out and on the street while I put my key in the lock, turning to wave at her a little. She didn't notice.

I sighed. What a life this Willow had. I felt a little sorry for her, which is to say for myself, and walked into the house. It was cool and quiet. I felt the air conditioner come on. I looked over at the thermostat, which was on the wall near the stairs, and saw how low it was. I considered turning it up, but then knew I'd have to face the explanation later. In my pre-wish house, we always had the temperature set as high as we could stand so that we used less energy.

I climbed the stairs quickly after that, not even thinking about grabbing something to eat. I opened the file on my computer labeled "FGR.doc" that told me everything about being a fairy godmother, and started reading.

I skimmed several chapters but wasn't finding what I was looking for. I decided to use the find option, and typed in "memory loss."

I was immediately taken to a long paragraph on exactly what that could mean.

"Memory loss on the part of the granter means they inadvertently granted a wish that should never have been granted. Finding a senior or full-blooded godmother is imperative, as the longer the wish remains granted the more difficult it is to reverse. If the granter goes on to grant another wish, then the original wish is irreversible, no matter the consequences."

Great. I was almost feeling a sort of wish pressure. I could hope that it was too soon, but you never knew.

Even so, at most, I probably had no more than ten days. I needed to find out more now.

I looked up what a senior or full blooded godmother was. The senior godmothers were anyone who had been a fairy godmother for more than five hundred years. I thought about the group I met with and I wasn't sure if that fit any of them. It struck me then that perhaps there were multiple groups. After all, it wasn't like there were all that many of us.

A full blooded fairy godmother was a person who was born a fairy godmother. And here I thought such things didn't happen. I tried to find out more but there wasn't any information in the rule book. I had no idea how to contact anyone from the group. I looked up emergency contact but there wasn't much information. My head was starting to hurt. I laid it down on the desk for a few minutes, but I must have dozed off.

Chapter Four

"A Fairy Godmother cannot grant their own wishes."

—from the Fairy Godmother's Handbook

I started awake. My room looked like it had before, the lavender and black stripes, but no purple. There was only the soft hum of the air conditioning and the click of ice in the refrigerator. I listened for any sounds from my brother's room, but heard nothing. I was probably still alone in the house.

I looked at my phone. I had only dozed for about half an hour. I had so much to think about and figure out that I was surprised that I could sleep at all. But I had been exhausted since granting this wish. Maybe that was it.

It took me longer than it should have to remember what I was doing. I tried to trace back my thoughts but I kept forgetting things. Finally I started writing things down. Clearly I couldn't trust myself to remember. Just as clearly,

I needed help. I didn't have a way to contact other fairy godmothers in my group, but I had to figure something out.

I knew names, but not areas. It's not like we kept up with each other on Facebook. Most of us don't have much in common. In fact, it was my understanding that most of our group didn't even live in the same country. Which meant this could be a tough search. I only had the full names of a couple of people to start with.

Paula had been nice to me from the very beginning. I knew her last name was Sayers so I started plugging that into search engines. I found a profile on Facebook. Fortunately she hadn't hidden any of her photos, and it was the Paula I was looking for. I sent her a PM, hoping that it would reach her, as we weren't "connected".

Then I sat and waited. I tried playing games, but it's hard to concentrate even on stupid, mindless games when you know your entire world is at risk. After about five minutes, I figured I should see where she was. She was on the west coast which meant that her time zone was about three hours behind mind. It would still be early. Hopefully I caught her before work. Hopefully she checked into Facebook regularly.

I scanned her timeline. Yeah, she posted most days. So if she looked at my message, she could respond. The big question was would she see my message?

I got up and paced. My stomach still hurt, but at least I was doing something. It was like I had this sudden realization that I had to do something *now*. I wanted to wish but I knew I couldn't grant my own wishes. I also knew that if I granted a wish for someone else that this meant I'd be stuck here in this post-wish world.

Suddenly I didn't want that. I mean, I have issues with my real mom and her worry. In fact, I pretty much have issues with everything about my real life. Sometimes Sage drives me insane, but she's my bestie. I didn't want to lose all of that because someone else wished something bad. If I hadn't been the person granting the wish, would I even have known? Now that scared me and made me really sad.

Then I got scared that maybe Paula wasn't still a fairy godmother. What if the wish had changed things for her *and* me? Maybe we weren't even connected through the fairy godmother group and she'd just see my email and think it was some crazy kid pranking her? What if she tried to get me tossed from Facebook?

So I worried about that while I paced. My stomach started to hurt even more. It started to feel all butterfly-ish, like I was nauseated, too. My pre-wish mom, not this one, would have worried herself sick over me and the way I was feeling. She wouldn't have left me alone in the house to stew on my own. She would have hovered. She would have been searching for home remedies. She may even have called our naturopath.

In some ways, maybe it was good that pre-wish Mom wasn't here. But I wanted someone to comfort me. I needed to talk to someone. I considered whether it would help to bounce to the room where we all met. I decided if I didn't hear from Paula in the next hour I'd try that. Maybe there was some sort of alarm and someone else would show up?

I could hope but I didn't want to get them too high.

Forty five minutes later, I still hadn't gotten a response. I ran into the bathroom, practically ready to vomit, but nothing, just the feeling that I could vomit. When I came back and glanced at the computer there was a message in my box. I checked it. *Paula.*

I'd told her that I thought I had granted a bad wish and that things had changed. I told her I could only remember a little bit of it, but that I thought someone had wished their brother didn't exist.

Paula's reply was quick and to the point. I was to think about the basement and meet her there as soon as I got her message.

I grabbed my wool socks and sheerling slippers and tried to picture the basement. It took me a while to focus. I brought up the damp smell, the wet drippy sounds. I imagined the sofas. I felt the chill damp that always seemed to be down there. I felt the springs in the horrible chair poking my butt. I felt my feet getting colder. After what seemed like hours, but was probably only a couple of minutes, my bedroom finally started to fade out and I popped into the basement.

Paula was already there. She's a bit younger-looking than my mom, but definitely an adult. She tends to wear sweater dresses and leggings, and today was no exception, although her sweater was short-sleeved and light and her leggings were a mushroom color. She was wearing heels rather than slippers, too.

"Thank god," Paula said. "Tell me all that you recall."

I rushed over to her, avoiding the largest of the puddles.

"I think it was my friend Ashley. She's really different. All Goth, and she's not at all my friend any more. I had this thought that I remembered her brother being at a barbeque at my house, but she doesn't have a brother in this world. For some reason I think she wished him away!"

Paula nodded. "Things have felt off for me. Nothing like that, mind, but just as if things aren't quite right. So we need to find a senior godmother, or a full-blood, but I've never met one of them. I'm not even sure who qualifies as a senior. Carl, the guy who made you a fairy godmother, was getting close, but not only was he burnt out, he didn't want the extra responsibility."

"Don't we have one in our group?" I asked.

Paula shook her head. "Seniors have their own meeting places and times."

"But if we need to find one, how do we do it?"

"We wish," Paula said. "Let's hold hands and both say it. We'll wish that we could talk to a senior fairy godmother. Just keep repeating with me and we'll send all our focus on that wish okay?"

I nodded.

I took Paula's hands. They were cool but slightly damp as if she were worried about something. I wanted to pull back and wipe my own, but really, did it matter? I held on.

"I wish to talk to a senior fairy godmother," I said. Paula's voice echoed with mine. We chanted that phrase about a dozen times. Sometimes our voices were stronger and sometimes weaker. I felt like I was a witch doing a spell. I sort of wished I had the kind of power to make something like that work.

Then something popped and there was a young woman, not much older than I am, standing there. She was dressed in open-toed high heels and low-slung pants. A tank top showed off a narrow band of belly. Her hair was brown, streaked with purple, and cut in one of those styles with the front and sides longer than the back.

"What did you do?" she asked, not even looking around. It was like she knew this place. Maybe she did.

"I think I granted a wish that shouldn't have been granted. I sort of think someone I know had a brother but now she doesn't. Everything is all weird."

"Come here," the senior fairy godmother ordered. That was it. She ordered me. Like I was her slave. Well I needed something from her, so I didn't let myself get pissed about it and walked over to her.

Paula just stood there, watching. I hoped she stayed. I really didn't want to be alone with this girl that I didn't know, although given that she had to have been a fairy godmother for at least five hundred years, she clearly wasn't actually a *girl*.

I stood closer to her. She smelled normal, like a young woman. There was a hint of perfume, which probably meant it was more expensive than what most girls my age would wear, but it was the kind of basic faint scent we'd aspire to as we got older. Not that my pre-wish mom wanted me wearing scents and stuff, but, you know.

Her skin was pale cream and completely perfect. Like I ever had skin that clear. I wondered if mine would clear up at all as I worked at this or if that kind of skin was something you got when you got to be a senior. If so, that could be so worth it.

"Quiet your mind," the girl said.

I wished she'd just stop ordering me around. Naturally I had a hundred things to think of that had nothing to do with her. Quiet my mind. How did one do that?

I tried to think of white but then things kept moving around in there. My brother playing in a snow. A white paper falling from my desk at school a few days ago. My mom painting the black lines in my room while I painted the purple on the other side. Then I smelled the paint and the thick paint fumes wafted over me. I felt nauseous again.

"You think too much." The girl walked away from me, pacing the floor. "What will help you stop thinking?"

I shrugged. I mean I'd never tried to not think.

"Don't they teach you how to focus here?" She looked at both me and Paula.

We both sort of shrugged. Clearly Paula hadn't heard of this before.

"How senior are you?" She was asking Paula.

"I've done this for about twenty years."

The girl smirked a bit. "And you?" she looked at me.

"About six months now."

She rolled her eyes. "Figures. It's always the newbies who get sucked into this sort of wish. I've told them a hundred times they need some sort of training, not just a rule book, so that you can learn not to hear those wishes, but the full-bloods think it's just fine as it is and no one listens to me."

"There's *training*?" I asked. It was sort of like finding out that you could get scholarships to be a cheerleader, like Lauren's mom wanted her to get. I mean, come on. Everyone wants to cheer, but who thinks of getting paid for it for college? And when you find out, things sort of click into place. Training would have been awesome. Maybe I wouldn't keep getting sucked into thoughts that I didn't really want to hear.

"No." The girl said. "But there should be."

Paula and I looked at each other. Paula was starting to look decidedly uncomfortable. "So do you have a name?" she finally asked the senior fairy godmother.

"I go by Brin now," she said. "Everyone laughs when I say my real name, as it's rather out of fashion."

It occurred to me that if I lasted doing this for five hundred years people might think Willow was a strange name.

"Paula," Paula said holding out her hand. Brin looked at it but didn't immediately grasp it. Paula let her hand drop, awkward. "This is Willow."

"Like the tree?" Brin asked, looking at me.

I nodded. Great, she had an issue with names. She raised an eyebrow but said nothing.

"Well Willow, let's see if you can sit in one of those chairs over there," she pointed at our eclectic collection of chairs and our one sofa, all in brown and more brown, some more crap-colored than others. "And then I want you to close your eyes and focus on your breathing."

I wandered over to the end of the sofa where there was actually a comfortable spot. Paula took a seat on one of the other chairs, far enough away that she wouldn't interfere but close enough that she'd hear everything. She had an eagerness that made me suspect she loved being part of something unusual. Like this was her life. What sorts of weird stuff could we get up to as fairy godmothers? Great. She'd probably be gossiping about what went on soon enough. Only to the group, of course, but I hated the idea that someone would be talking about me when I wasn't there. Except I would be there, wouldn't I? But it was the fact that she wanted to gossip that bothered me.

"Close your eyes," Brin said again.

I did as she asked.

"Now focus on breathing in."

I did so.

"And breathe out," she said, a little later than I wanted to breathe out, which kind of interrupted my breathing pattern.

We spent some time getting synchronized with her talking me through breathing in and breathing out and me doing what she asked when she asked it, not a few seconds before or after.

"Now, I want you to think only of breathing in and breathing out, as you've been doing," Brin finally said.

I started thinking that I was breathing in and out. My mind wandered to wonder if scuba divers did this to stay calm. Then I pushed that thought aside. I had a moment to feel proud of myself that I did that, thinking my mom, who was always into meditation and thought I should be too, would have liked that. But then I was off thinking again and I brought myself back to my breathing.

Finally things faded around the edges and I woke myself up with a soft snort. I opened my eyes without thinking, but Brin was smiling a little bit.

"Seems your mind is just as active when you sleep."

I shrugged. I mean, I guess. Wasn't that a good thing? It meant I *had* a mind and I was exercising it. Okay, I'm not that dumb. I know that we're supposed to be able to control our thoughts and calm down with meditation and stuff like that, but it really wasn't something I was good at. I mean, I'm a frigging teenager not some monk in a cave, right?

"But fortunately I was able to glean that your hunch was right. Your friend Ashley did wish she'd never had a brother, and that is the wish that split the timelines."

"What does that mean?" I asked. "And what do we do?"

"It's not what *we* do," Brin said. "It's what *you* get to do."

Great. I have to grant a wish whether I want to or not, and now I'm the one who has to clean up the mess?

"What do I have to do?" I wasn't thrilled about it. Hopefully it wouldn't be too hard, like clearing my mind.

"Listen well, Willow," Brin said looking at me carefully. "I'll write down what I say so you won't forget, but you need to remember as much as you can, okay?"

I nodded, not sure what she was getting at.

"The more you remember of the old world, the stronger you'll be when you go to undo the wish, do you understand?"

That made sense so I nodded.

"That means you need to work on remembering everything you can about your life and Ashley's life before the wish. Remember her brother. Can you see his face?"

I tried. There was a flash and then it was gone. It was a strange sort of sensation like knowing you knew something but not being able to find it. My mom had that problem with words sometimes. Usually my dad was around to fill in the blanks for her. Or I was. Or my brother. We laughed at her for that, like she was getting old and we weren't. But here I was, doing the same thing with the face.

"Let me help," Brin said.

I got a clear picture of Ashley's brother's face. Of course. A thousand memories came flooding back of seeing him in the halls, of my brother being annoyed because he always had to tag along with him, acting like equals, whenever our families did things together. It brought back times when Ashley, Sage, Lauren, and I had all hung out and had fun. Ashley could be a major witch sometimes, but she was my friend.

I realized her wish had always been her wish, even if she didn't say it. Her folks had wanted a boy. She was supposed to have been a boy but she'd been a girl. They'd doted on her because her mother had had a hard time getting pregnant, but when she was five, her mother finally had another baby, and that was the hoped-for boy. All of the doting went away. Ashley had to help do this and that and the best of everything always seemed to be reserved for her brother.

In some ways I'd always envied her because she got away with a ton of stuff, but now I saw the problem. No one came to her basketball games when she played, but her folks always went to her brother's events, even though some of them had to have been boring. Like science fair? Yawn much?

I felt sad for her. I remembered hearing her wish, wishing myself that I hadn't heard it when she wished it. Then things changed. I saw, and sort of felt, the world tip. Even Brin held out a hand, like she was unsteady on her feet when I remembered that. I heard Paula gasp a little as it changed. The water dripped to the side rather than straight down and then the world was upright again.

"Wow," I muttered

Brin smiled. "It was a big wish and it has bigger implications for later on, too."

I could only imagine. I wanted to ask what those were but I had a feeling that wasn't something I was supposed to know.

"I couldn't tell you if you asked," Brin said. "I can see some of it, but only a full-blood godmother could see all the outcomes and all the implications."

I nodded.

"Now, you'll need to do that kind of memory while you're with Ashley. Then you two need to wish for a full-blooded fairy godmother. Take her to your bedroom, okay? It's probably easiest if you do it there. I can be sure to be there to boost your wish."

"Wait. Wait." Brin made it sound like it would be easy for me to get Ashley to my house. "Ashley and I don't exactly connect in this world."

"Then connect." Brin made it sound easy. She was the lovely mean girl on the shows, acting as if because it was easy for her, it should be easy for all of us, except that it wasn't. I sighed.

"I'm not sure I can. I mean, I think we're sort of enemies this time around."

"Then un-become enemies," Brin ordered. "This isn't

a rule I'm making up as I go along. You both have to be there. You and Ashley need to talk about the brother you remember, so that she starts to recall such a brother. Then you need the full-blooded fairy godmother with you. It's not easy to get their attention, so I'll be there to help— they'll listen more to my call than just yours, no matter the reason."

I nodded. "I'm just saying, it won't be easy."

"Could she make a wish to make it easier? Like could she wish that Ashley comes by?" Paula asked.

"Do you have a wish building?" Brin asked.

Paula shook her head. "No but I thought maybe you…?"

Brin shook her head. "My wish granting was coming to see you so I'm all out. To find another, we'd need to wish for them which would take care of that. It's sort of tricky. I suppose she could *hope* someone hears her, but you know how it is. There just aren't many of us, and there are so many wishes. Although some of us listen carefully and try to grant only the good ones."

Brin sighed watching me, as if this was somehow my fault. I mean, how stupid is that? We're not trained. I'm a kid and I've only been doing this a few months. Okay, I hear a lot of wishes, right? It's not like I made a choice to grant this one. Believe me. I didn't. I'd felt badly that I heard it. In fact, I kind of tried to go elsewhere but the wish push was there and Ashley really wanted her wish. I had felt that, even though I knew it was wrong.

"Look it's not like I wanted to grant that wish. Maybe you should tell the full bloods how useful some training would be."

"Someone would have to do the training," Brin said. "And unless someone steps up to do that, it won't happen. It took centuries to get the darned rule book copied. The only reason it's online now is because someone had a scanner and was techy enough to want to play with it."

I nodded. At least they had people like that. Some people who were clearly more forward-thinking than others. Of course if the seniors were all over five hundred years old, well that sort of meant that new technology and stuff was probably hard to keep up with. Five hundred years ago, I thought. Did they even have printing presses in Brin's day?

Brin took my hand. "Let's go back to your room. Focus on it."

I did so and pop. We were there in my room. Paula hadn't come with us. No doubt she was sad that she had to go back to her ordinary life. On Monday, our usual meeting day, she'd probably want to know all about how this had gone.

Chapter Five

You can't tell anyone you can grant wishes."

— from the Fairy Godmother's Handbook

B rin pulled out a report, surprisingly detailed, of all that I had said about Ashley's brother. She even had an image of him, almost like a picture, but it was clearly hand drawn, like a line image in color. I wanted to ask how she'd done that, but I didn't want to annoy her—Brin seemed like she was the sort to be easily annoyed about things she thought I ought to know.

I wrote down what I remembered and listed the things I had to do. I had to befriend Ashley, like right now, today, and get her to my room. I checked my cell phone. It was almost two. School was out at two thirty. Ashley was two bus stops up from my house. I might as well go up there and wait. Hopefully she'd be on the bus.

"I should go and try and find Ashley," I said.

"I'll be here," Brin said. She was looking around at the room, taking in the lavender and black stripes. I wondered if Mom and I had painted those together or if she'd been too busy with her work to help out. Maybe I'd done it all. Or maybe Sage, or perhaps Cherize, had helped. It made me sad to think that all those memories of my mom weren't true for me everywhere, you know? I hated that she could be so different from world to world.

"It's funny how little things can make such big changes," Brin said, like she was reading my thoughts again.

"Like?" I asked.

"Getting a job. So that you're too busy to think about the things that give you real pleasure. Instead you spend time trying to make more money. I imagine most of the changes in your life are because Sage's mom didn't get the job at the dentist's office and your mom did. Not that Sage's mom has done anything different. She got a different job because that's who she is, but your mother... well, she isn't quite the woman you knew, because she got distracted."

That was interesting.

"All because Ashley didn't have a brother?"

"Ashley's mom was the one who helped Sage's mom get the job at the dentist's office. She'd been the receptionist, but once she was pregnant with her son, she wanted to quit. In this world, Ashley's mom left the office for a higher level position and didn't recommend Sage's mom. Your mom applied and got the position. So here we are."

Well that made sense in a weird sort of way. And I was kind of feeling like an extra in *It's a Wonderful Life*. Of course, how exactly did Brin know all of that?

"No angels get their wings here, I'm afraid," Brin said,

grinning at me. "Now I think you should get going, in case the bus is early or something."

"Do you, like, read minds?" I asked. Because this was getting way too weird.

Brin just gave me a long look and said nothing. Even though it totally creeped me out, like there were bugs-running-all-over-my-clothes-and-I-couldn't-see-them   kind of creeped out, I didn't know her well enough to push her. But it was too weird that she just knew what I was thinking. If she registered that thought, she didn't say. Naturally. Because it seems like no one ever wants to help. Note to self: telepaths are not helpful.

Although I doubted the bus would be early, because let's be real, I hurried out of my room, surprisingly unconcerned about leaving Brin alone in my room. I mean she was a five hundred year-old senior fairy godmother. I'm sure if she wanted something, she could get better things than I had. Still, it felt weird to leave a stranger in the house when no one was there.

I hurried down the walk, hoping that Mom's job didn't end early, but I'd gotten the impression she worked a full day, so I should have until five or so. Dad wasn't as keen on the yard work, clearly, so perhaps he had less time because Mom had less time. I walked up the street. The day was clear and sunny. I didn't need the jacket, like I had thought.

I walked quickly past the houses. A dog barked. A white Toyota sedan drove down the street, but I couldn't see who was driving it. It wasn't my post-wish mom, that much I knew. She had an SUV. Which was way too weird to think about, really, so I didn't.

I looked around. Everything looked mostly normal. The house on the corner was nicer than it was in my world. I wasn't sure who lived there, but clearly something had changed for them, too, or maybe a different family had moved in. Who knew how those things worked?

I climbed the slight hill that would take me up to the road that Ashley lived on. She was two blocks from the bus stop, but I figured I didn't have to hang out at the stop. Her family lived in a slightly fancier house than mine. It might be just around the corner, but the builder here had clearly had much more grandiose ideas. The houses all had a slight push out on the garage and there were fancier porches, as if we all lived in the old South and not the edges of Charlotte. Which, I suppose at one time *was* the old South, but not any longer.

There was this one house across from Ashley's bus stop that had columns that made it look like a miniature Tara or something. When I saw the movie, *Gone With the Wind*, this was the house I thought of. Ashley had laughed at me. Although she admitted it was probably true enough. Her mom loved that house. In fact she said her mom was reading the book when she was pregnant with her.

"It's one good reason not to be a boy, I guess," pre-wish Ashley had said. "Imagine being called Ashley as a boy *now*."

I wondered if we would still have talked about that in this world. Would that have been a forbidden discussion? I waited outside, sitting down on the sidewalk, putting my feet out in the street. It was warm sitting on the cement, warmer than I expected. I was way too early. Three cars drove by. One woman in a gray mini-van stopped across the street, just down from the bus stop. She glared at me as if I were some troubled kid about to cause problems. Hopefully her child would be long gone before I stopped Ashley.

I sat there, playing with a leaf that had fallen towards the gutter and considered how I would approach this. I had to get it right. After all, Sage would be on that bus, too, and I thought we were still friends, even if we weren't all that close in this world. I mean, we still sat together, right? Really, I might miss my pre-wish mom, but I would really miss pre-wish Sage if this didn't work out. I had to make sure Ashley came with me.

I heard the bus long before I saw it. Then I smelled the diesel fumes of the gas and heard the air puff of breaks as it turned onto the street. I stood up to wait. I saw faces looking out of the bus. I wasn't sure I recognized everyone, not that it mattered all that much. I was looking for Ashley. I didn't see her face in any of the windows. I did think I saw Sage, but I wasn't sure. She was talking to someone on the bus. Thankfully, if it was Sage, she didn't appear to see me.

The woman with mini-van waited and picked up two kids who were slightly younger. She had them get inside her vehicle. She was starting her car, but was still watching me. Ashley was the last person off, and started to walk down the street. I followed her, calling her name.

It took her a moment but she turned, slowly, wary.

"Can you wait up for a moment? I'd like to talk to you," I said.

The mom, clearly not worried about a girl dressed in Goth black, watched us, made a frown, but left with her two kids.

Ashley waited for me, not saying a word. At least she wasn't running down the road screaming that I was a bitch and to get away from her. I mean Mini-van mom probably would have put a major stop to that right away, leaving me with some major explaining to do. I suspected that should that happen, Brin was not going to be a big help, or any sort of help at all.

The street got quiet around us as the bus turned down

the road away from the direction Ashley was heading. Her house looked pretty much the same. They had a wisteria growing over a large arbor along the side, which they didn't have in my world. The wisteria did cut down the yard a lot, meaning that Ashley's brother would have had a smaller area to play in. Maybe that was why?

"What do you want?" Ashley was still standing in the street, making no move towards her house, or towards me.

"To talk, like I said." I tried for confidence, but I was feeling anything but. Still, Willow always exuded confidence, and even this Ashley would know that. If she saw me stammer and worry, she might think she had the upper hand and do something stupid. Or just delay things and make life even more difficult.

"Why would I want to talk to you?" Ashley asked. Her voice was harsher. Normally she had this sing song lilt in her voice, but this voice, well, this voice was harsh. Like she was used to telling people off.

Now the Ashley I know is no shrinking violet. She can be harsh, but this girl was *cutting*. Pre-wish Ashley had a fine tuned sense of how to cut people down without them ever knowing she was cutting until afterwards. This was not that.

I shrugged. "Why wouldn't you?" As soon as the words were out, I hoped she didn't answer them. I wasn't sure I wanted to know.

Ashley surprised me by laughing.

"Figures Willow Vaughn can't even consider why someone wouldn't want to talk to her."

"Oh come on. I didn't mean it like that. I did need to talk to you about something, and it hopefully won't take too long."

Ashley gave me a funny look. Her body was turned half towards her house and half towards me. She moved a little here and there like she hadn't made up her mind, but she wasn't leaving.

"Have you ever thought about having a brother?"

Again, a laugh, but this was a short harsh laugh, like it was a horrible idea; like I'd struck her with something painful, and likely I had.

"Like it's up to me?"

"Maybe it is," I said.

Ashley shook her head. "You don't get it do you?"

"Get what?"

"I do this because I'm supposed to *be* the boy. That's all my parents wanted, but there was no boy. They're stuck with a girl and they hate that. Especially my father. Why am I even telling you this? Why do you even care?"

"Because I think as much as you hate the idea, your life might be better with a brother."

"Yeah, well, medical science can only go so far. If there have been break-throughs, I'm pretty sure I'm not the one who made them, you know?"

I shrugged. She was right.

"I have a friend that I'd really like you to meet."

"I am so not falling for that again," Ashley said and started to turn further towards her house.

"Wait! It's not like that," I called. I hated that my voice shook a little at the end. I couldn't let her just walk away. She needed to come with me.

Ashley paused and looked at me.

"Like what's up with you? This ain't the Willow I know and definitely do not love. You on the outs with Sage and Lauren, and you think your life is over if you don't play this prank?"

"It's not a prank. It's weird. Nerdy weird and I can't explain it, but my friend can. The worst that will happen is that someone will see you walk into my house. Believe me, I'm hoping Sage *doesn't* see that."

Ashley gave me a long look, measuring me, weighing.

I wanted to say something else, but I had a feeling the fact that I didn't want Sage to know she was coming by was a hook. I'd gotten her curious.

Then, "Nah." She turned and walked up to her house.

Chapter Six

"If you grant it, it's your responsibility."

— from the Fairy Godmother's Handbook

"Really?" I called. "That's it? You won't even talk?"

Ashley turned back to me and walked up close to my face. "When was the last time it was just 'talk'? Like the time you and Sage invited me to sleep over and then took all those photos of me drooling and plastered them everywhere?"

"It's not a sleep over. Just an hour or two. To meet my friend, Brin."

"Why is it so important to you that I meet your friend Brin? Is she gay? Cause I'm not. Even if I was, I wouldn't want you to know." Ashley made air quotes around the phrase "your friend Brin" as if she didn't want me to think she believed me about having a friend.

I shook my head. "It's not that. She just needs to talk to

you. She's at my house. I don't know why she wouldn't come with me. She can explain this all better than I can. It's just too weird."

"Why does she have to explain anything to me?"

"Because I think you made a wish and that it turned out to be a disaster."

Ashley nodded again, not smiling. Then she rolled her eyes, shaking her head side to side, like she couldn't make up her mind about me.

"You're a piece of work, Willow."

"Come on. What can it hurt? I promise I won't take any photos and I won't tell anyone. We can sneak in through the backyard. Whatever makes you comfortable, but will you please come talk to Brin?"

"What's she going to do if I don't? Kick your ass? Cause I might like to see that."

I sighed. I tried to keep from rolling my eyes, but it's sort of a reflex in certain situations and this was one of them.

"Well how would you see it if you don't go?" I asked. It sounded reasonable to me.

Ashley didn't see it that way. She just shook her head again and turned.

"Oh come on," I shouted. I didn't care who heard me, which is a huge big deal because that is like so overly emo. And I don't do emo. I stay cool. Logical. Reasonable. But not now.

Honestly, I think I was just plain scared. After all, if this didn't work out, I could be stuck here. I definitely did not like this life better than my old life. Like if I could have not granted this wish, I would *so* not have granted this wish.

It was enough to make Ashley stop and glare.

"Look, I'm not asking for a ton of your time. The only person that should be there other than the two of us is my friend Brin. She's a little strange but she's not like someone from school who's going to take photos of you using my bathroom or something sick like that."

Ashley watched me carefully. There was a part of her that wanted to say yes, but there was another part of her that didn't trust me at all.

"I'm not going to take a friggin video of you doing something stupid, okay? I'm just not that interested."

Ashley laughed a little. With that she turned back towards me and walked slowly up to me.

"Just not that interested huh? I'm not even good enough to be picked on by the great Willow Vaughn?"

"Not in this world," I said. After all, in the pre-wish world, she was one of my friends. In fact, she was one of the few friends who had major issues with my new nicer personality. I mean granting wishes feels really good and when you feel really good all the time, it's hard to maintain that sort of cynical personality that I've always had. So yeah, I was changing. Ash didn't like it one bit. Neither did Lauren, but I understood Lauren a bit better. Besides, Lauren wasn't here having this conversation because she didn't have a little brother she'd wished away.

"What world would you want to make fun of me in?" Ashley asked, like she actually expected an answer.

"Maybe a world where you could see what a dork you're being," I said.

Ashley glared at me and started to turn away.

"I am so not going away." I followed behind her. "I'll stand at your door and annoy your entire family until you come with me."

"I heard you went home sick," Ash snarled. "You get some sort of mental disease and become my stalker?" Her hands were on her hips.

"Not quite why I was sick," I said. "That was physical.

But it's gone now and I *will* follow you. And I will bang on your door and keep banging on your door. And I will embarrass the heck out of you if I have to. But if you come with me, I'll leave you alone. In fact, I'll promise not to do anything to embarrass you for a month if you'll just come with me now."

I hoped a month was enough for Ashley. I mean, who knows what I was getting up to in this world. Still, there was something in her eye that made me think she might go for it.

"Three months," she said. "You don't bug me for three months and you keep Sage off my back, too. And if you hear Lauren is planning something, you give me a warning. Doesn't have to be public. You get a black ribbon or something and flash it on your purse if there's bad crap about to happen."

I nodded, agreeing. I hated to think of what post-wish Ashely was going through. It seemed like she just expected people to be mean to her, which kind of made me sad. Pre-wish Ashley was a lot of fun. Annoying sometimes, but still a lot of fun. This girl didn't seem to know the word.

Ashley made a face but she tromped down the street, away from her home. She had her back slumped and she put both hands in her pockets, which is so not how the Ash I knew walked. Still, she was coming with me. I hoped I wasn't smiling too big because that would so not be me. Even the new and improved Willow who granted wishes didn't smile like that.

Chapter Seven

"It's better to not grant a bad wish than to try and correct it."

— from the Fairy Godmother's Handbook

We got to my house. I glanced across the way, but I didn't see Sage anywhere. Ashley was looking around at our house.

She looked at the cherry tree and snorted. I was tempted to say something but decided against it. I noticed that she looked very carefully at everything around the front, as if she were looking for traps. Considering what little I knew of this post-wish Ashley, that could totally be true.

I had my key out and opened the front door. Inside, Ash paused in the entry area. It's a small area that's raised up from the dining room on the left and then there's a hall that goes to the back of the house. There are stairs in the middle, leading up to my room. Ashley stood there looking around, taking in the beige carpet and the dull beige walls.

I hadn't noticed before but the dining room table was plain, without the nice place mats and vase pre-wish Mom always sets on it. There aren't usually flowers, but there could be. Pre-wish Mom always says that it's about the intention, and her intention is to make dining together a pleasure because there is nothing more basic than eating well. Yeah, right. Whatever. We still usually eat in the kitchen. But it's the intention, right?

It bothered me that something so obvious had been overlooked. I led the way upstairs. Ashley followed, looking around like someone who had never been in a house before. I wanted to say something snarky but being so close, I didn't want to lose her trust and have her bolt out the front door. Or demand something of me that I knew I wasn't going to give if I got stuck here.

She eyed the walls and the closed doors, even the open bathroom door, with the wariness of a dog that was just waiting for the vet to come out and give them a shot, or worse. She looked about as human as that dog would have looked too. Really, there was real fear in her eyes of what was coming.

Ashley wasn't someone I normally would have called brave, but I had to raise my estimation of her in that moment. She was doing something she really did not want to do, but she was going anyway. I wondered if that sort of gutsiness carried over. It also made me wonder just how important that three month truce was, and what sorts of things Lauren and Sage had been doing to her. And me. I mean, I was here. What kinds of things had I done? I suspected they weren't very nice.

My room was in the front of the house on the right, and my door was open. Brin was lying on the bed reading something, although I didn't see the cover. I didn't have any magazines up there, and I hoped if she was reading something of my mom's that she'd put it away before she left.

"We're here," I said. "Ashley, this is Brin."

Brin nodded at Ashley who looked her up and down and seemed completely unimpressed.

"You're older than I thought," Ash said.

"So she didn't tell you?" Brin asked.

"I figured you could explain it here. I mean you know what's going on better than I do," I said.

"No." Brin said. "This is *your* show. You need to convince her you need her help."

"What the...?" Ashley started, looking from me to Brin.

"Remember when I asked you if you had a younger brother?" I started.

"What is up with that?" Ashley's eyes hardened. She wasn't afraid any longer, now she was getting mad.

"Well you have one," I said. "In another sort of time-line, or universe, or something."

Ashley rolled her eyes at me.

"Anyway, you hate him."

"Now that sounds like me."

"You wished he'd never been born."

"Even better," Ashley agreed. Great she hated her younger brother even though he hadn't been born.

"Your life here sucks, doesn't it?" I asked. "I mean three months of knowing when Lauren wasn't going to play a prank on you or embarrass you got you to follow me here. But it's not like that in my timeline. In the world I know, I hang out with you, but you're the one *everyone* wants to be friends with. There is no 'great Willow Vaughn'. I hang out with Sage. You and Lauren are besties. You two rule. Really."

"Like am I cheerleader, too?" Ashley said. There was no mistaking the sarcasm in her voice.

"You don't dress all in black," I said. "No Goth-look stuff. In fact, you're the girl everyone wants to be."

"That has so gotta suck," Ashley said.

"Well, you like it. Except for your brother."

"So why would I wish him back?"

"Because I haven't seen you smile once in this world. You do that a lot in the other world," I said.

"How do you know my smiles are real?" Ashley asked. "Clearly I'm too uptight in your 'alternate timeline'." She even used finger quotes around the words 'alternate time-line' while rolling her eyes. What is up with that? I was starting to agree with my mom that eye-rolling and fingers quotes were ridiculous sometimes.

"I know they're real because we're friends."

"So you're all 'boo hoo, I've lost my friend Ashley, and I want her back'?" Ashley asked. She was standing there with her hand on her hip.

"If you want to believe that, go ahead," I said.

"I'd rather get it on film. Go ahead and cry about losing your good friend, Ashley. I'll put it up online and see how many hits I get."

I glared.

Brin was sitting on the bed, watching. Her arms were behind her back and she leaned her weight on them. She didn't say anything. I wanted to ask her for help, but she'd been very clear that this was something I had to do. Even if I was failing miserably at figuring out what to say.

"I'm not going to cry over losing you," I said. I heard something behind me and turned to see Brin spreading out the papers from earlier. There was the hand-drawn image of Ashley's brother.

"See?" I said, holding it up. "This is him. Your brother."

"Nice," Ash said. "Can I take this home for my mom? She'll love having a picture of her imaginary baby."

I sighed. "Look, just go with it. What can it hurt?"

"I don't know. How many social media sites are there where you can put up some video of me 'going along with it'?"

"She's got a point," Brin said from the bed.

I turned to glare at her. "Like, this is helping?"

"You're clearly not getting anywhere." Brin stood up.

"What do I have to say?" I asked Ashley. "What would make you believe me?"

"Like nothing?" Ashley said. "I haven't seen that person ever before. I don't want to. I don't want a little brother."

"She's right," Brin said. "Her life may have been better from your point of view, but in this world, she's content with the life she has."

I glared at Brin. "So now what?"

"You could get comfortable in this world," Brin suggested.

I shook my head.

Ashley laughed. "No matter how happy I might have been in your world, knowing how much you don't like this one is sort of worth it. Besides, a younger brother? That wouldn't give me what I want, but it would totally give my folks what they want."

"So you *do* believe in other worlds?" I asked.

"Heck no," Ashley said. "But I read. I know that people believe in them, and clearly you are having some sort of weird-ass break and think you know about one of them."

"So wanna play a game?" I asked.

"Not really." Ashley was starting to look at the door like she wanted to leave.

"Let's hold hands and say 'I wish for a full-blooded fairy godmother.'"

"You have got to be f-ing kidding me," Ashley said.

I shook my head.

"I so need a video of you saying that. Are you sure we have to hold hands?" She put her own hands up and then let them flip down.

"It won't work," Brin said.

"Why?"

"Because she likes this world. It's not right, but she likes it."

"So what do I do? How do I make this right?"

"You can go now," Brin said to Ashley.

Ash shook her head and left the room. "You still owe me," she said looking at me. "And if you don't live up to your end of our bargain, I will *so* use this against you."

I watched out my door as she tromped down the stairs. She was opening the front door when my brother came in.

"Whoa, Goth Princess."

"F you." Ashley returned.

I shook my head. Eric closed the door and I retreated to my room with Brin.

"So now what?" I asked.

"Now is the hard part."

Like getting Ashley to the house and trying to convince her to want her brother back wasn't hard enough.

Chapter Eight

"There are certain privileges available only to Senior Fairy Godmothers."

— from the Fairy Godmother's Handbook

"I wonder what made her hate her brother so much," Brin said.

I closed the door gently. I had no idea if Eric would come down the hall or play video games in the living room. I mean, he was and he wasn't my brother. I thought about Brin's question, thinking of the Ashley in my world. It was hard, because it was like there were holes in my memory where her brother should be.

"He plays pranks all the time," I said. "I can't remember exactly what, but some of them are really mean. I remember her crying a few times. And her folks…" I trailed off, thinking how her mom really never seemed to listen when Ashley had a complaint. It was like their whole world revolved around her brother, and Ashley was just a nuisance. Even I felt it, and I didn't live there.

I'd tried talking to my pre-wish mom about it a few times, but she'd said that there were people who just wanted something so much they couldn't see the people in front of them. She also reminded me why it was really important that when Ashley was around our house she felt welcome and respected.

"I think I like your other mom," Brin said, doing that mind-reading thing again.

"How do you do that?" I asked. This mind reading was so very, very creepy, but I had bigger problems.

"You're transparent." She smiled at me from over by the window.

"So what do I have to do?" I asked, wanting to get whatever task Brin was setting for me over with so I could go home to a pre-wish world.

Brin sat back down on my bed. She gestured to my desk chair so that I could sit down there, as if I needed her permission to sit in my own room.

"You'll need to find something from your world," Brin said. "Something that embodies your world as you know it, something that made it here unchanged."

"Like what?" I asked. I had no ideas coming.

"Some people find a photo that reminds them of the old world. Others find a rock or a leaf."

I thought about it. What kind of thing would embody my world? I immediately thought of my pre-wish mom and her obsession with food—organic, local food. I thought about her cooking, and plain yogurt, and the nice meals we'd have at home. I had a feeling dinner was so *not* going to be a nice a meal. I thought of the difference between our hybrid car and the SUV she drove now.

"I'm thinking at how different my mom is. I mean she's

really into organics and whole foods and stuff in the world I know."

"So maybe you try and find something that represents that to you," Brin said.

"Like what?" I asked.

Brin shrugged. "It needs to be meaningful to you."

I thought about it. I could find a coupon for some whole food-type thing or plain yogurt online. That would so be my mom. Or maybe I could go to the Farmer's Market where she always shopped on Saturdays. The wishing well that had made me a fairy godmother was there. The more I thought about that, the more it made sense. That market had made me who I was.

"I need to get to the Farmer's Market," I said. I had a sudden fear that it wasn't still there.

"The one with the wishing well?" Brin asked.

I nodded.

"Do you have a car?"

"I don't even have a driver's license yet," I said. I mean I'm almost sixteen and I have a learner's permit, but I don't drive yet.

"Too bad. That would make things easier," Brin said.

"Can't I just wish myself there?" I sort of hoped she'd say yes.

Brin shook her head. So now I had to get my butt to the Farmer's market. I sat down the computer, put in the address, and looked at the bus routes until I found one. I could make it to the first bus stop. It'd be late when we got back, but maybe we could do the work there so post-wish Mom wouldn't freak out.

"Can we work there or do I have to come back here?" I asked Brin. "I mean, if I'm gone after having come home sick, this mom is going to be like royally pissed-off at me."

Brin smiled. "Take the stuff there and I'll go with you. We'll ride the bus together. That should be fun."

I could only imagine that Brin had a majorly warped idea of fun. I slipped the papers and stuff into my backpack. I checked to be sure I had exact change for bus fare and then I got ready to leave.

"Do you have bus fare?" I asked her.

Brin nodded. "I'm sure I do."

Eric wasn't around when I left the house, but I didn't think too much of it. He was probably locked in his room or had gone over to see one of his friends. That was normal enough.

I locked up the front door and Brin and I walked down the street. We had to walk out of the subdivision to get to a main street for the bus stop. It was only a few blocks. I passed Sage's house but I didn't see anyone at home. Maybe she'd gone over to Lauren's or something.

Brin walked silently. She looked at everything. When a dog barked, her head turned in that direction. She turned when a breeze started blowing so that it hit her in the face and her hair blew back against it.

"Why do you do that?" I asked.

"Do what?"

We passed a small blue house that I didn't recognize. In my world, there was a larger house here, but I could see that this might have been the old house at one time. I wondered how Ashley's folks not having a son had influenced this.

"I like the wind. I like the feel of it. Dogs often bark because something is going on, and it's always good to pay attention," Brin said.

I had no answer for that. I kept walking. We passed the large brick sign with the name of our neighborhood on it, *Treacle Villas*, in tall black letters. I know, the world's most stupid name. I looked up 'treacle' once and it's a syrup made from sugar. I don't have a clue why an adult would want to live in a subdivision named after a syrup.

We turned right at the sign, staying on the sidewalk, considering it was late enough that there was a fair amount of traffic. It was only a few feet to the bus stop. There wasn't a shelter here. There was at the next stop a few blocks up, but that wasn't the safest place to wait, and my mom always said I should wait here if I took the bus.

We waited, watching cars pass us too quickly. I counted fourteen SUVs, none of which, fortunately, looked like my post-wish mom's. I switched to counting sedans to take my mind off of her and her SUV. I counted twenty, three of which were hybrids.

I got bored with that and started to fidget. Brin was standing near the edge of the curb hanging her head as far out as she could, probably to feel the breeze from the cars. It made me nervous and I wanted to scream at her to get away from the edge. I mean, she was my only link to my real life.

Finally I saw the bus slowly meandering up the road. Same air brakes hissing and spitting as the school bus. But this one slowed down faster and, of course, there were no signs for cars to stop. It also smelled more. Lots more gasoline fumes. The one good thing was that Brin backed up on the sidewalk as it pulled up.

I got in first and she followed. I paid my fees. Brin just waved at the driver, who seemed fine with that.

"What's up with the wave?" I asked.

Brin smiled. "Perk. Think of what you might be able to do in five hundred years."

I rolled my eyes. I know, watching Ashley do it, I was thinking how irritating it was, but really. There are some things that are worth the eye roll and this was one of them.

I mean, I would wait five hundred years to not pay a bus fare? Big whoop.

We rode the bus for about a mile down the road and made a turn onto another busy street. I watched people in cars speeding around the bus. I saw a car nearly slam into the back of us. I watched people get on and off. The guy with the pink hair was most interesting, as that's not something you see a lot around here. In fact, most of the people on the bus weren't people I'd normally see, because normally, for all her talk about environmental responsibility, I ride with my mom in the car if we go someplace. We rarely rely on public transportation.

After we rode about half a mile down another main road, passing several office buildings, we got off the bus. From here, we could wait on the corner for another bus or walk the mile or so up this road and be at the market.

"Let's go," I said, walking.

"Really?" Brin asked. "It seems like no one walks anymore. Not like in my day."

"Let me guess. You had to walk ten miles to school in six feet of snow, uphill, both ways."

"Actually," Brin smiled. "We were lucky if we had a school, so we didn't complain. It wasn't that far either. I lived in a small city."

I nodded and prevented myself from rolling my eyes—which is really hard to do when it's become a habit—and didn't say anything else.

It was late afternoon and warm outside. Traffic was picking up. A steady stream of cars passed us, and we were briefly treated to a mix tape of music that was played loud enough to be heard over the engines of a passing sports car. Brakes squealed in disharmony when they came too quickly to the stop signs. Like didn't they see the sign before? Does anyone pay attention when they drive? Maybe I should take the bus more often. It might be safer.

Brin didn't say much, looking around her. There were plenty of office buildings, which is kind of weird when you think about it. I mean we were on our way to a Farmer's Market so you'd think that it would be out in the middle of farm land, but not this one. No, it's near the commercial district, where people do business-type stuff like computers and banking and crap.

At least everything looked pretty much the same as it had when I came here with my pre-wish mom. If it hadn't, we might really have been in trouble, because I doubted Brin would be any help in getting us there, even if she did have special perks and powers.

Some trees had been planted on the space between the sidewalk and the road. Probably to keep the drivers from accidently plowing into pedestrians. Trees are hard to miss. On my other side there were lots of beige brick buildings that stood between three and five stories high. About halfway down, a set of red brick buildings appeared, in case one got bored looking at all the beige buildings.

Across the street I saw apartment buildings in gray and white, brown and white, and one in white and red brick with fancier balconies. That gave way to a field, which is really what you expect before you get to a farmer's market.

It seemed like the walk was longer than it had looked on the map. I can't say I've ever walked it before. Mom drives us here from the other direction, but when you take the bus you don't really have a choice. It seemed to take forever to get there, but *finally* I saw the sign. The iron parking gate was closed, meaning they weren't even open. Still, it's open land, and Brin and I walked around parking gate and into the market proper.

There's one fully enclosed area and then several

covered sections. Beyond all that is a brick patio surrounded by grass, and beyond that is the little area with the wishing well. There was a nice breeze there, and I thought Brin had the right idea to enjoy the wind on her face. It felt good after that walk on the street. Here, at least, it didn't smell like exhaust.

I guided us to the wishing well, relieved to see it. Even the usual bench was there with its lame-assed heart-and-rose in wrought iron on the back. It smelled like the bamboo that waved in the breeze behind the bench. I sat down and pulled things out from my backpack. I wondered what would be the perfect symbol from here.

I thought about a bamboo leaf, but rejected that. Too small and not really how I thought of this. I could grab a rock but rocks meant nothing to me.

"I'll be right back," I told Brin.

Brin was looking at the well. She just glanced at me and nodded. I walked over to the building and looked around. There was a flyer about the market on a bulletin board near one of the main doors. I pulled it down and brought it back to the wishing well.

"Will this work?" I asked, holding up the flyer. "It feels right to me."

"Then let's give it a try," Brin said. "You might want to sit down. You'll be closing your eyes and concentrating again."

So there I was, sitting on the bench in a posture that mimicked my first encounter with a fairy godmother—although that time someone else had been using my bench, forcing me to pretend to wish. What a mess that had made.

Chapter Nine

"Full-Blood Fairy Godmothers should only be called in greatest need."

— from the Fairy Godmother's Handbook

Brin sat next to me and held my hand. It felt a little weird at first. This was a wishing well, and I knew that people often came here to sort of be alone, or rather alone together, if you know what I mean.

"Close your eyes," Brin ordered.

I did so.

I thought about my breathing, hoping that would start to quiet my mind, given that I had a feeling a quiet mind was going to be a big part of what I had to do.

"Now," Brin said, her voice was more modulated and quiet, sort of like someone doing hypnosis in a movie. "I want you to think about your life, your world. Hold onto that piece of paper. Remember this place and what it means to you. The organic, environmental aspects of this place that your mom, your pre-wish mom, loves."

I did that. I thought about my life in the real world, the world where I was annoyed by my parents, but where I knew what to expect. I thought about all the times my mom had hovered, worrying. I thought about how frustrating she could be when she was certain I had eaten something I shouldn't, which was nearly every day. I heard her singing *"A Whole New World,"* when I was complaining about having to start something new. It was all there.

I dream-smelled bacon and eggs, which of course she bought from the Farmer's Market, so the eggs were fresh laid from pastured chickens and the bacon came from happy pigs, so that made it happy bacon, I guess.

"That's good. Keep those thoughts. Bring in your friend Ashley, the one you knew there. See her happy."

I thought about that. What made Ashley happy? I remembered a skating party when we were in elementary school and she was laughing. She had to have been happy more recently than that?

I had to push through some images of her being frustrated by a math test and rolling her eyes when I said something about people getting their wishes, 'cause you never knew. Wink. Wink. You know?

Finally, I got something. We were at the mall. Her mom had dropped us all off and we were getting clothes for school. So it was almost a year ago, but she'd been really happy then. We were all excited to start into high school.

"Finally!" Ashley said, "High school!"

"I need to make sure I try out for cheer," Lauren said. "My mom thinks that's a really under-utilized scholarship, particularly if I do really well in classes, too."

"I hope that we meet some of the cute guys from

Killinger," Sage said. "They had the best looking basket-ball team."

Sage and I had been stat girls for the basketball team at our middle school. We'd seen some of those guys, and she was right, they *were* cute. But were we cute enough for them? It would depend upon the girls who went to school at Killinger Middle School and what they looked like.

"Let's head in here," Ashley said, pointing to one of the big outlet stores. She turned and plowed into an older guy carrying a coffee. He moved the cup aside so that he and Ashley didn't get hit with the hot liquid. He success-fully avoided getting any on Ash, but some of the coffee splashed on him anyway.

Ash had turned and apologized, but he'd just made a face and walked on past a movie poster for a Disney re-release of Aladdin. Then she'd giggled. I know it sounds bad, but I also know she was totally nervous about the acci-dent. She probably felt silly, too. We'd all looked around to make sure no one had noticed her accident. I mean the guy was old. He had gray hair, a beard, and stood barely taller than we did. He wasn't fat but he looked like the kind of guy who would play a serial killer in one of those crime shows – you know, one of those guys that no one ever notices?

Naturally I mentioned that. I mean I wasn't as nice as I am now. That made us all laugh. Ashley most of all.

"Good job," Brin said. "Keep going with that. What did the mall smell like?"

Once again, Brin was reading my mind.

This wasn't just about what I looked like when I was thinking. This was mind reading. Apparently when you get to be a senior, it's something you can do but I still didn't like it. I'd been avoiding thinking about her ability, wanting to just get this over with but it was really weird now that she wasn't even covering that she was reading my mind. What else did she know? I started to go down that road but then pushed it away. No sense letting her in on all my worries, concerns. She'd be out of my head faster if I did what I needed to do.

The mall had smelled of coffee. There were people talking, but it was hard to hear any particular conversation. It was just that low drone of voices that came from everywhere and nowhere. The coffee smell was from the spill that had made Ash laugh, of course. There was also a faint smell of popcorn from a vendor down near the food court and the stronger smell of French fries from the same direction. There was also the faintest smell of bleach and baby diaper, which meant we were probably close to one of the family bathrooms. Thinking about it, we probably were. It always stunk in there, even when they had just removed the 'closed for cleaning' sign.

I focused on the scene as hard as I could, pulling all the senses together. We'd all laughed while we walked into the store Ashley had wanted to go into. She'd been checking her top to be sure there wasn't any coffee on it. We were all in shorts and t-shirts over tank tops that had built in bras. Lauren had slightly larger breasts so she had a real bra on under all of that with the bright red straps showing under her white tank and navy t-shirt, color coordinated, as always.

"Wish that Ashley could be that happy again," Brin said softly.

I wished that Ashley would be that happy again. Of course, beneath that was the hope that I'd be that happy, too. Ashley wasn't the only one unhappy in this world.

"Now wish for a full-blood fairy godmother," Brin said.

I wished for that.

"Say it out loud."

"I wish for a full-blood fairy godmother," I said.

"I wish she could grant your wish, because I can't," Brin added. "A full-blood needs to grant this girl's wish."

Brin now had both her hands placed on mine, clutching me as if she was afraid that if we lost our grip we'd be pulled apart in space and time or something. I mean, it was really beginning to hurt. And her nails. Had she never heard of trimming them or filing them? Cause it felt like she had cat claws.

I was starting to really wish for the full-blood fairy godmother to come. I mean, my hands felt a little damp now, and I worried that it was because Brin had drawn blood. I had an image of blood running down my arms and dripping on the ground. Someone would find me here later on, maybe not until tomorrow, and I'd be dead because all the blood from my body had been drained out. Then there would be this massive search for a serial killer that they would never find because she was a Senior Fairy Godmother.

"Stop that," Brin whispered.

There she was reading my thoughts again. It was one thing when the thoughts pertained to my wish, but another when she was just randomly reading my thoughts.

I opened my eyes because I was planning on telling Brin to stop reading my thoughts, but the world had gone all sort of purplish-blue and there was a fog of some sort. Then things tilted. That's the best I can say. Imagine riding in a boat and a wave comes up and the boat leans over and just stays there. That's how the world felt.

I started to smell citrus and grapes. Grapes, of all things! Grapes are okay, but I hate grape juice, although Eric loves it. I hate the smell of it. So I wrinkled my nose.

Then I heard a sound like someone had dropped an

airplane on the ground. There wasn't any smoke, but the fog dissipated and a man walked out.

He looked more like someone auditioning for a cheap cop thriller than a fairy godmother, if that's what he was. What is it with me and male fairy godmothers? Creepazoid Carl had been the one to grant my wish that got me into this mess. Maybe I should have wished I never made that wish at all. But then I started thinking about everything I could lose.

"So you granted a bad wish?" the guy asked. He had a sort of low-key kind of British accent, but very minor, like he'd lived in the states forever.

"I did," I said.

"What do you want to do about?"

"I want it undone." Like wasn't that clear?

"But the one who made the wish isn't here. Is it still her desire to have that wish?"

I looked at Brin.

"Umm… she wouldn't really talk about it. But she seems really unhappy?" So there, that was a try.

I looked at Brin who shrugged. She seemed really uncomfortable.

"What do you think, Senior?" the man asked.

"I believe the girl who made the wish is very unhappy. She's one of those girls who dresses up all in black and wears funky makeup. According to Willow, in her pre-wish world this girl is very popular; but here she seems to have no friends," Brin said.

What about the fact that she'd told me that this was a bad wish and things needed to be changed? What about that? Why didn't she say that?

"So if I send you back, she could easily wish again and you might end up granting the bad wish once again," the man said.

"Can we make sure she doesn't?" I asked, hopeful.

"No."

I could have used a name for him. I mean, Cop guy was too generic as he wasn't even in uniform. It's just that his hair was a little messy but short and he had that sort of law and order look about him. Kind of ageless, too, when you think about it. I mean, if I passed him on the street, he's totally the guy you'd completely forget you'd ever seen. I don't know what I was expecting but this was so not it.

"But you can be trained to not grant a bad wish again," he said. "So before we reverse your wish, we'll work on training."

Chapter Ten

"Every Fairy Godmother has a unique way of granting wishes."

— from the Fairy Godmother's Handbook

S o there I was, by the wishing well at the Farmer's Market, working with Brin and the full-blood fairy godmother. He told me to call him George. I had a feeling George was not even close to his real name. But whatever floats your boat.

I spent a lot of time with my eyes closed. I was supposed to be centering my thoughts. Now and then one or the other of them would send an "I wish" through the air and I'd hear it. I was supposed to work to not hear it, but that was hard. It's like sitting next to someone playing the trumpet and being told not to react to them blowing the thing in your ear at random intervals. It is just not easy.

And honestly, this was all so woo-woo meditation-y that

it made me miss my mom, the one I wanted to go back to. That made things even harder, because my mind kept wandering even more.

"You need to concentrate, Willow," George said. He was standing by the fountain, leaning back against it. He had on black trousers and a button-down shirt in the palest gray, which I think is what made me think he was on a cop television show. They often wore that sort of 'business casual' look, or whatever it was.

"I'm trying. But this is hard."

"A child should be able to do this," George said.

I opened my eyes.

Brin was pointedly not looking at either of us and I was certain she was working not to roll her eyes, except when does a five hundred-plus-year-old roll their eyes? Maybe she was young at heart, right? Or more likely, I was imaging it, or figuring that's what she was doing when she was doing whatever it is five-hundred-plus-year-olds do instead of rolling their eyes.

I wanted to ask what he thought I was, if not a child, but, really, I couldn't get that out of my mouth. I don't care to be called a child any time, but compared to people as old as the two of them, well, okay, 'child' might fit. I just could not get my mouth to make the comment. I went back to trying to focus. They played trumpet in my mind a few more times.

"Maybe this will work better," Brin suggested. "Try to focus just on your breathing, like you did for me earlier. Then focus on your favorite song tune."

So I did that. At first it didn't seem to make any difference. I tried to remember a favorite song, but there were a bunch of them and none of them wanted to stay in my mind. What was worse, I kept thinking about pre-wish

Mom singing *"A Whole New World."* That got that song stuck in my head, which was something I *so* didn't want. It made it harder for me to focus on my own music. That meant every "I wish" jerked me out of whatever level of meditation I had achieved.

Finally I just went with the *"A Whole New World"* song and meditated on that. It was kind of like having to meditate on Brussel sprouts, but at least there wasn't another song trying to jump in and change the tune. Still, a trumpet blaring in your ear is a trumpet blaring in your ear, no matter what you're pretending you're listening to, but after a while it started to work.

In fact, it wasn't half an hour later that they both said, out loud, "I wish" and I hardly noticed. I mean I could have been texting with a friend when my mom said I needed to go wash my hands or something, it was that sort of "So what" moment. Naturally a few seconds later I realized I hadn't even noticed and then got all excited, which didn't excite them as much, but I could tell that Brin, at least, understood my sudden exclamation.

George made me do it again. Twice. I wasn't to break concentration at all. Can I tell you how much I was beginning to hate *"A Whole New World"*?

"I told you they should all get some training," Brin said when they let me stand up and walk around to work the kinks out of my neck and my back.

"As if we have the time," George said.

"Did you really have the time right now? When she needed you? Or was it just me sending up a flare about a clear need so you didn't have a choice?"

George shrugged. "Even Seniors don't get that much of a say."

George said it mildly, but Brin glared as if he'd shouted at her. There was clearly more to fairy godmother politics than I was aware of. I had a ton of questions I wanted to ask, but more importantly I wanted to get home. I wanted to undo Ashley's wish.

"Is there anything else I have to learn?" I asked.

George glanced over at me. "No."

"Can we undo the wish I granted?" I asked.

"You must swear that you will never re-grant this wish, ever. On pain of death," George said.

I felt something tingle around my body. When he said that, he meant it. I had a feeling I would die if I accidently re-granted this wish. I was so tuning Ashley out. In fact, as soon as I finished high school, I was moving as far away from her as I could, just to be sure.

"A drop of blood will seal the deal," George continued. He now had a small knife in his hand, all silver and black and it looked very sharp and pointed. It was sort of a cross between a knife and a tiny ice pick, actually, the blade was so narrow and almost round.

"I swear never to re-grant this wish," I said.

George took my hand and brought down the knife. There was a sharp sting, almost like a bee, and then there was a drop of blood, which he wiped away with his finger. He held that up to the air. A breeze floated through the little clearing where we were, next to the wishing well and that was that.

"Now we can reverse this," George said.

I waited. Did I need to vocalize the wish? Did I need to do anything? I was prepared to do whatever it took.

"I need you to walk around the well counter-clock-wise," George told me. I took a moment to pretend the well was a clock, just to make sure I went the right way, and then walked around it. Don't judge. It's hard to picture that sometimes, you know?

I returned to him and he was smiling.

"Is that it?" I asked.

"No," he said.

I wanted to ask what was next, but Brin spoke up.

"Stop playing with her," Brin warned. There was an edge to her voice, like she didn't like this at all. It was the kind of voice you expect from your mom when you're edging towards a big dog that doesn't look at all friendly to anyone but a three year-old. Ask me how I know that.

Yeah, I was that three year-old. To this day, I swear that dog was smiling at me, but my mom was certain he had rabies and was just waiting to take off my arm. My dad wasn't there but since I wasn't hurt—just a bit traumatized by Mom's reaction—he thinks she just read Stephen King's *Cujo* at a very impressionable age.

I tried to get her to watch the movie with me once, but she refused. After that, I've always thought my dad was right. So maybe the dog *was* just smiling at me.

I saw Brin glaring at me now, not just at George, so I pulled myself back to the present and looked at the two of them. George looked much less happy about her interference, but maybe this was more interesting to him.

"Don't even go there," Brin hissed. She was standing closer to me than I had thought.

George was smiling again.

"Can I go home now?" I asked. I put my best whiny girl voice into that.

George sighed and made a bunch of hand gestures. I thought that was strange. Wishes just flow from me, but this was like he was doing something with his hands, cat's cradle in the air or something, and then there was more fog and he was gone.

I heard cars on the street. The day seemed cooler than it had a moment ago. I smelled something damp and wet.

"We're back," Brin said.

"That was it?" I asked.

"For now," she said. "You aren't completely safe here until you grant another wish, so keep your head down. Remember the music thing we did. You'll need to use it."

Chapter Eleven

"Wishes have consequences."

— from the Fairy Godmother's Handbook

I had my cell phone in my back pack, so I took a chance and called my mom. She was totally confused as to why I'd gone out to the Farmer's Market when it wasn't even open.

"It was a school thing. I had to go someplace alone— someplace I don't usually go, so I could see how much easier it is to get to by car," I lied. I thought it was a pretty good lie. The only problem was that my mom is the sort of mom who might check into why a teacher might give that kind of homework. I wasn't at all certain what class this would be for.

Fortunately, she didn't ask. It was getting dark, after all, and there were clouds here. Apparently whether or not Ashley had a brother influenced the weather. Brin smiled when I thought that and shook her head. So there was more going on than I knew about.

Maybe there actually *were* parallel universes and that one had existed for more reasons than Ashley's wish, but just happened to be one where Ash's brother had never been born. That would explain some of the other little changes I had noticed. Of course, that begged the question of where the Willow who lived in that world was. Because people had known me there, but I wasn't there—unless I'd gotten sent here, but that would make no sense right?

"So what happened to that world?" I asked Brin.

"I have to go," she said. "It's a long story. Remember, keep your head down. Don't you dare re-grant that wish, because you *will* die and it won't be a pleasant death."

"Is any death pleasant?" I asked.

"The full-blood fairy godmothers have rather bloody ideas about death. You won't want to go that way," Brin assured me. "Make sure that you keep your mind focused on *this* world so you don't slip over there. That's a possibility, too, until you grant another wish."

"No one said that!" I yelled. I could slip away from this world into the other one? How horrible would that be? I was cold in my t-shirt. This was not appropriate wear for this world, not now as the sun was setting.

"The full-bloods forget to explain things. Honestly, George was getting sort of hungry-looking, and I needed him to un-grant that wish before he became all unglued."

I gave her a long look. "What exactly are they?" I asked.

"Nothing you need to worry about for another five hundred years. By that time, you'll be sort of immune. Just keep your head down. Be really thankful to be back here. If you feel anything strange, concentrate on all the things you love about being here, okay? And if you start feeling the need to grant a wish around your friend Ashley, focus on that song you were focusing on." Brin gave me that long, adult, eye-contact-you-heard-and-understood look.

I nodded. This was important. I needed to be thankful that I was here. I was cold and shivering, but I could be thankful that I had a mom who would come running. That felt good because that was my real mom. *My* mom, who asked very few questions and was just going to drive out here and pick me up unlike the mom in the other world. I was glad that this was my world, whatever that meant.

Brin smiled. "That's right. Focus on this world."

"Will I ever be able to read minds?" I asked.

Brin shrugged. "Depends upon how long you want to stay a fairy godmother. I love granting wishes, so it's been worth it to me to try and adapt, although I'm not always good at it. I only came up with the name Brin last year. I stuck with Hilde for too long, and people found that strange on a girl my age."

I smiled. So her real name was Hilde.

"I was born Brunhilde," Brin said, smiling again. "But there aren't many girls named that any longer. So I shortened it."

"Wow," I said. I wondered what kind of name I could make out of Willow if I lasted that long. I mean would people still be naming their kids after trees then or what?

"Don't even think about it. You can't even begin to imagine the future. I know I couldn't," Brin said. "Hopefully I won't have to see you around again."

"Is there a way I can call you if I get back into trouble?" I asked.

Brin sighed. "I wouldn't be able to help if you do. Remember to focus on how much you love this world, right now. Right here."

"One last question," I added, as she turned to leave. "Is it the same day and time?"

Brin nodded. "You didn't lose anything. People probably didn't even notice you weren't at school because the universes always make sure life remains consistent. Some might think you were sick. Just act like that was it."

Well if it was a parallel universe that still sort of existed, that made no sense at all. But Brin had told me not to think about it too much. And thinking about it might loosen that anchor that held me to this world. I *so* did not want to go there, so I did my best not to think about it at all which was best done by distracting myself from what I really wanted to think about.

"What about Ashley and Cherize?" I asked. "Will they remember things?"

"Ashley might. But I doubt that someone as normally removed from your social circle like Cherize will remember. If she does, it would probably feel like a weird dream."

I nodded and then waved. Brin turned and then she parted a couple of really tall bamboo stalks like she was parting a shower curtain, walked through it, and disappeared.

It wasn't long before my mom pulled up next to the closed-off rail by the Farmer's Market and I got in the car —the nice, small hybrid that was pretty basic inside because, after all, she didn't work and cars were expensive.

Chapter Twelve

_____

"Full-Blood Fairy Godmothers take agreements seriously."

— from the Fairy Godmother's Handbook

Mom and I got home without incident. Dinner went well. Eric was being really annoying about a computer game and I found myself wondering about him in the other world. My stomach clenched. I forced myself to find something to be thankful for about him in this world.

Yeah, that was about as easy as it sounded. I had to go through all sorts of things that I knew about him. I finally figured that at least he didn't bring friends home all the time and left me alone in my room when I wanted him to. So I focused on that. Because I could. My stomach felt better.

Still, I picked at my food during that time, which perked up Mom's worry mode.

"Are you feeling okay?" she asked.

"Just a little punky all day," I said. "Mostly okay though."

"You should have had a jacket. What were you thinking when you left this morning?" she asked. Fortunately, she wasn't really expecting an answer so I didn't have to give one. I wondered for a second what she might think if I did try to explain it to her.

She came around the table, the kitchen table, not the dining room table with all the place mats and stuff, just our plain, old, round, wooden table that sat in an alcove off the kitchen, and felt my forehead.

"You don't feel warm." There was worry in her voice.

"Probably because I'm not real sick?" I suggested. "I just don't feel great."

"Well, if you're coming down with something..." she trailed off and moved back to her seat. She sat on the side closest to the kitchen where it was easiest to get out. Dad had his back to the kitchen, and Eric and I were seated with our backs to the windows. I was most fully with my back to the windows because Eric watches a lot of cop shows and plays a lot of cop video games and he hated to be in that spot. Too easy to get shot at.

Thanks. Now I'll be the first one down. Not that I was really worried about some bad guy shooting us while we ate dinner.

Anyway, I continued picking at the gluten-free pasta and spaghetti sauce. Homemade by Mom, of course. It was Friday, so naturally she'd found something easy to make. At least it was easy enough for my dad to have watched it while she came out to get me.

That was something I was grateful for. I was glad that she was my mom, and not that other woman who would no doubt have gotten angry with me for ruining her scheduled time by being out in the middle of nowhere.

Eric and my dad chattered about the computer game he was busy with. I ate mostly in silence, but paid enough attention so that my mom wouldn't get super worried. Still, once dinner was done, I hurried back up to my room.

Sage and Lauren had both texted me during dinner. I am not allowed to use my phone during when we ate, which kind of sucks sometimes. Considering the alternative, it was kind of okay. I texted them back once I was upstairs.

"Are you okay?" Lauren asked.

"Feeling better?" came from Sage.

So I *had* been out sick.

"Yeah." I texted both of them. "Better."

"Good. We're still on for tomorrow?" Sage asked.

We'd been planning on a movie—her mom was going to drive us. A bunch of kids at school were talking about seeing it, so who knew who else might end up at the show.

"I'm good." I typed.

So that was that. My life was my life again. I was really glad that my Sage was back, too. I liked this Sage. The girl in the other world was strange. She clearly liked to play games with people. It made me wonder a little bit if the Sage I knew might want to play games, or maybe was playing games, pitting Lauren and me off each other sometimes. I could see that now. It was something to be aware of. Still, this Sage had always chosen me as a friend over Lauren. I wasn't sure about the other Sage.

It was weird to think about that as I texted online back and forth with both of them. Ashley came on a little later. It turned out her brother and a couple of his friends would be at the movie tomorrow, too. It annoyed Ashley and she wasn't pleased.

I focused my mind on music, although that immediately pulled me into the earworm of *"A Whole New World."* Ugh. Then I focused on all the things I was thankful for in this universe. Fortunately Lauren typed something else at the same time as Ash, which changed the subject, and I didn't have to deal with it any more. I hoped that I would get a wish pain soon so I could feel more secure here.

Still the world felt funny for a moment, like the air was harder to breathe and there was a funny smell. The colors in my bedroom seemed muted and my stomach started to hurt. I focused on being thankful for being home, my real home. I was thankful that I had a friend like Sage. I was thankful that I had a friend like Ashley. My room came back into focus and the colors shifted to the darker colors that were in my real room. The smell left me. My stomach still hurt a little but even that was fading. I took a breath.

I checked other social media sites, reading what my friends had been up to. I read notes on my wall and private messages here and there. It helped me piece together what had gone on while I was busy fixing the world. At least I had only one day to figure out and not an entire life! I spent a moment being grateful for that. Because you know, just in case.

Chapter Thirteen

"There will always be another wish to grant unless you decide to no longer serve as a godmother."

— *from the Fairy Godmother's Handbook*

The next day, Sage's mom dropped us at the theater. We all had our own stash of cash for lunch, the movies, and a snack later on. The theater was in a complex that was part of an open air mall, one that had started out as an area of big box stores that had gotten popular. The real mall was up the road a bit, but this was a great place to grab a quick bite to eat and do some window shopping.

We wandered down past the row of buildings along the wide brick-paved sidewalks. There was a popular restaurant that we liked this way, and we all decided that would be a good place to eat. Inside it was crowded, as always, but we got a table without having to wait. The movie wasn't for another two hours so we could have waited a little, but who wants to?

I ordered a burger and fries. It was one of my favorite things because my mom hated it when I ate fries. She thought they were full of transfats, unless of course she made them with special oils and stuff. I guess she was magic or something. Lauren ordered a burger with a salad and Sage had a wrap and soup. Ashley also got a burger and fries.

It was one thing I liked about Ash. She and I both ate what we liked. Granted, we had good metabolisms so it never seemed to matter that we ate a fair amount. My mom always said it was because I ate healthy food, whatever that was. We were all laughing and talking about what we'd see.

"Oh my gosh," Lauren said. "Is that Jason DeMaio?"

We all looked. Ash had been crushing on Jason for the last couple of months. He appeared to have noticed and spent some time at school talking to her.

"Stop it," Ash snapped. "He's coming this way." Her seat faced Jason. He stopped at our table and said hello. He and Ash talked about the movie we were all going to see. He was with a few friends, and unfortunately there was no way they could all join us. I was both disappointed and glad. I had enough on my plate without worrying about how I came across to one of the boys.

Ashley and Lauren giggled for a little bit. Sage just smiled, a little superior. She'd been fantasizing about Doug Layton, the quarterback for most of the year. He hadn't noticed her, but Ian Wells, who was a junior, certainly had. He wasn't in the group, which was unusual, but Sage had told me that he'd talked to her about being gone for the weekend. His folks liked to camp up in the mountains.

Sage liked Ian well enough and she wasn't about to

turn him down, even if Doug was the one she really liked. In the other world, she'd practically ignored him. I had to wonder if they'd gone out or something. I wondered how she had gotten to the place she was in in the other world, game playing and super popular.

My stomach clenched and my breathing got difficult. The table seemed a little less solid and it looked like Ashley was dressed in black. I made myself focus on the fact that I was glad to be there with Sage, Lauren, and Ashley and that they all liked me.

My stomach still hurt and while the black seemed to dissipate around Ashley, like she'd shaken off a shadow of the Goth clothing, the table was still a little less solid than it should be. I reminded myself to be glad that I was getting to sneak French fries and that my mom wasn't around to complain. I thought about how much her complaining meant, particularly when compared to a mom who didn't care.

No change. If anything, I thought Lauren was starting to glare at me and Sage was starting to look at me like I was a bug. I mentally tried to focus on music and how much I liked music here. I mentally tried to recite a few words of my favorite songs but they weren't coming to me.

Instead, yep. You got it. I was able to picture my mom singing *"A Whole New World,"* sticking the blasted song in my head again. This was so not the life-changing earworm I wanted.

Finally the world righted itself and solidified. Lauren and Sage were looking at me, concerned. Ashley was solid and dressed in a blue shirt, without a black shadow hovering around her. I took a deep breath, then sipped my soda, the real stuff. I'm not supposed to have it at all but sometimes I sneak the real, full-sugared thing. No diet drinks for me. My mom would flip. Well she'd flip either way, diet or no, I guess. Just because that's my mom. I made a mental note that I was glad she was.

"Are you okay?" Sage asked, watching me. "You looked really pale there and seemed to have a hard time breathing."

"Just for a moment," I said. "But I'm okay now."

"Are you getting asthma?" Lauren asked. She liked knowing symptoms for a lot of things and was always inquiring with a specific diagnosis, as if she knew anything.

I shrugged.

"Your mom won't be pleased," Lauren said. "Sudden onset can be a sign of allergies, so maybe it's something you're eating?"

Lauren and my mom. Great. They were both food police. But Lauren got the same thing at home so I wasn't really surprised. Sometimes her mom made my mom seem almost normal.

"If it keeps up, I'm sure my mom will do something," I said.

Our food came while we talked. We all dug in and ate at our various paces.

"I hope my brother doesn't completely ruin this movie," Ash said. "I've been looking forward to it."

"We'll make sure we don't sit near him," Lauren assured her.

Sage and I nodded our agreement, me with a fry in my mouth.

"Yeah, but you know him. He'll probably move mid-movie or something." Ash was starting to get a little upset.

Her brother really can be annoying. The fact that her parents always wanted a boy means that he never really gets punished for bothering her. No one stands up for Ash. At least if Eric were as bad as Ash's brother, my folks would be all over him. Of course, Eric is older than I am, so that means he's usually pretty decent. He takes his responsibilities seriously.

Once, walking home from the bus stop, some of the kids in Eric's class started calling me names, and he went over and yelled at them. He nearly got into a fight with one of the boys. He avoided it, but they knew never to bother me again. He kind of liked being a sort of hero. Although, he teases me a lot.

Of course, at home, I've kicked his ass a few times when he got out of control. He thought I wouldn't be able to hit very hard, but he learned quickly that I'm a not a weakling.

Anyway, no one stands up for Ashley. Her brother dripped ketchup on her favorite blouse, one that was still fairly new and she'd saved her allowance for months, and no one said a word. It was clearly not an accident, because the blouse was in her closet. She cried for I don't know how long. He just laughed.

Her parents said that accidents happen. Apparently, they somehow believed he was accidently in her closet with a bottle of ketchup. Oops. Sorry. Thought you were the kitchen and had my burger! Nope. Not buying it.

My brother would have gotten in *so* much trouble. Of course, that *is* a sort of little brother thing and not a big brother thing, unless, I guess, the big brother was really immature. Fortunately for me, that wasn't true of my brother, however annoying he could be in other ways.

At any rate, that's life. But, yeah, we did have something to worry about with Ashley's brother.

I pulled myself back to the table again with thoughts of how grateful I was to have these people in my life. I had an older brother who I liked. I had parents who cared. I had friends I liked.

My centering didn't help Ashley though. She was still on a roll.

"I can't believe he has to come to this movie. He knew I was going, of course—I bet that's why he wants to see it. He totally thinks movies like this are stupid. I mean, he's not old enough to really enjoy it. But he got a friend to agree to come along and my mom can't say no, so he'll be sneaking around. He'll probably ruin it for all of us."

We all made nods and sounds of agreement and solidarity. I tried to remain thankful. I was grateful I had friends that trusted me to listen to their angst, right? Of course I was. I said that until I could feel it, although my stomach was knotting up and I got a glimpse of sad, Goth Ashley.

"I wish he'd never been born," Ashley cried.

I spent a moment being grateful that she was my friend. That I was still there. That her wish hadn't immediately transported me to the other world. Although, the room dimmed. Breathing was hard to do. In fact, I felt kind of faint, it was so hard to breathe.

I smelled a horrible smell, like burnt meat and skunk stink. I grabbed onto the table. I could barely feel it, like my hands weren't really my hands, but I made myself be thankful that the table was there to be grabbed and that I could hold onto it.

This so could not be happening. I mean I didn't even feel like I had a wish to grant, right? I started mentally singing *"A Whole New World,"* not because I liked it but because it was the only song in my head. It reminded me of my mom, always telling me that I should take on new challenges. She would prep me for things, telling me that I was good enough for whatever I was worried about. She made change seem like a fun thing. Which was probably not something I should have been thinking about in the midst of almost being thrown out of a world I didn't want to leave.

I thought I heard people saying my name. They sounded a long way off. I heard something that sounded like a wave crashing, drowning out their voices.

Ashley, Goth Ashley, bent over me and she was smirking. She gave a little hand-wave like she was totally loving this moment. I closed my eyes, focusing on Ashley in blue. I focused on how much I liked my friend Sage and that she was my best friend and had my back.

I was still mentally singing, fortunately too breathless to even accidentally hum, "*A Whole New World.*" Which I so didn't want because, darn it! I was thankful for that old world. Where I knew history and my teachers and my brother and Doug Layton hung out and farted around down in the basement, sometimes really literally.

I got a breath, finally. I was thankful I could breathe. I was still at the table with Sage and Ashley and Lauren. I reminded myself to think thankful thoughts for that.

I really was thankful I was still there. Was I going to have to avoid Ashley for the next week or so in order to avoid such a thing happening again? I hoped not. We hung out a lot and I had a limited number of excuses. Of course, I could pretend to be sick for a week, and then I wouldn't see anyone.

"Are you okay?" Lauren had her hand on my shoulder. I became aware of it about the time I heard her speak.

Maybe I wouldn't have to pretend. Maybe they'd all believe I really was sick.

"Yeah. I am now. I felt like I couldn't draw in a breath," I said.

"Maybe we should skip the movie," Sage suggested, looking worried.

"No. We just sit there. I think I'll be okay," I continued.

"But it's not like we'll be able to see you in the theater," Lauren pressed. "You could sit there dead for the entire movie and no one would know."

"Wouldn't that be creepy?" I laughed, to lighten the mood. I argued my way out of the whole we-aren't-going-to-the-movie thing, although it came up twice more. Fortunately, Ashley didn't mention her brother again, at least not while we were eating.

Chapter Fourteen

"The need to grant a wish can come on suddenly or slowly"

—*from the Fairy Godmother's Handbook*

We were fine in the movie. I mean once the previews started, we weren't really talking. The theater was comfortable and familiar with seats so old and worn you had to be careful not to get a broken one. That was especially true in the middle, where some leaned way too far back. There were a lot people from my high school there, so the theater was crowded, which meant that there were people who weren't Ashley's brother sitting right behind us.

Troy, her brother, could still try and be annoying, but he'd gotten there late enough that he couldn't get that close. He tried to persuade the people next to us to move so he could sit with his sister, but given that we wouldn't vouch for him, well, they really weren't willing to do so.

I made it a point to think about how grateful I was that there were people like that around us. And that Troy was late.

So I sat there, surrounded by the scent of popcorn, which I wasn't having, and soda, which I was, even if it was my second. My mom would freak if she knew how much of it I was drinking. But hey, that would give her something normal to freak out about. And wasn't I glad to have a mom who freaked out about my diet and health?

The movie was good and there were no little brother pranks. We saw Doug Layton coming out of the theater, but he and his friends had been sitting way in the back and Lauren doesn't like to sit there. The air conditioning gets way strong back there and you pretty much need a coat in order not to freeze. The boys like it though. My brother usually goes with them, but he was doing an extra credit project for a computer class because he is like, *so* into computer games, which meant he didn't come to the movie. Brothers! I reminded myself that I was glad to have him.

"So what did you think?" Doug asked Sage.

"It was great," Sage said. She gave him a smile. "What about you?"

I tuned them out, smiling a little at Lauren and then at one of Doug's friends. I forget what his name was. He was nice and not bad-looking. I mean a girl's got to keep her options open, right?

We talked a little, passing the theater posters, three Disney re-releases, and some movie about a guy making a wish that goes badly. I shivered thinking I knew that one all too well. Then we heard an angry scream from Ashley.

"You little creep," she screamed. "How dare you?"

She was dripping wet and the drips were faintly brown. No doubt Favored Brother had dumped a soda all over her

—which was pretty obvious since he was standing right next to her with a soda cup tipped over in his hand.

"What happened?" I asked. Lauren and Sage stopped. So did the boys.

"I wish you had never been born. Do you know how you've ruined my life?" she screamed at him.

I felt a pressure building, like I needed to grant a wish. Oh no, no, no. I started thinking about my songs. My favorite songs. The words wouldn't come. Just the whole blasted *"A Whole New World"* song.

Still my world felt like it was tipping. The pressure was still there, so I hadn't granted the wish, but I was going to need to grant one soon. I hated it when it came on quickly. Now was *so* not a good time to have to grant someone's wish.

I couldn't see anything for a moment and my breathing stopped. I was in my own little meditation cocoon, except that this wasn't really normal.

I couldn't breathe. I could barely think and I couldn't see but I thought my eyes were still open. It was just black.

This was way worse than what had happened earlier.

My stomach was clenched tight, and I was holding onto wish power with everything I had. I wished then that I could make a wish to get rid of the power.

Ashley was still screaming at her brother, completely unaware of me.

Someone was touching me, at least I think so. The hand was there and I let myself be grateful for it. It had to be a friend, like Sage or Lauren. I was really, really grateful for both of them for being my friends.

I heard the vague words, "I wish…" but I tried hard to push them away. The wish power was really pushing. My stomach was knotted and hurting, sharp and aching, like someone was cutting me from deep inside. The wish power was pushing to get out. I felt like I was in the movie *Alien* with one of those creatures trying to cut its way out.

"Willow? Please? Wake up. I wish this weren't happening to you," Lauren cried.

I wasn't completely sure that was a good wish, but there wasn't any negative feeling like I got when it was a bad one. I let the wish power go, feeling relief flood through me.

My pink wish cloud floated from me and the darkness receded. I was sitting on the ground and I was gasping for breath, which felt really good. Lauren was standing over me, Sage and Doug were looking at me. The cute guy, Darren, I think, was kneeling next to me. I wasn't looking up at anyone, because I was just sitting there like I had sat down on the ground, rather than fallen.

I was thankful for that, given that the cement was hard. Ashley was still swearing at her brother, which also made me thankful. While I think I had granted Lauren's wish, I wasn't going to push my luck. I planned to spend the next month or so being thankful. Just in case. That was too close.

"Are you okay?" Lauren was practically crying.

"I think so," I said.

She smiled.

"Don't ever do that again."

"Everything just got black," I said. "I couldn't see."

"All we saw was that you looked over at Ashley and then you just sat down on the ground," Darren said. "It was kind of like you were doing your own sit-in against her screaming at her brother."

"Maybe I was," I said, letting him take my hand and help me up.

I was pretty sure Lauren's wish had worked. I was really thankful for Lauren for making the wish when she did. It might have been a lifesaver.

Chapter Fifteen

"Granting a good wish feels good."

— from the Fairy Godmother's Handbook

I made it through the rest of the weekend okay. Finally it was Monday night, which meant that it was meeting time. Yep, Monday at seven, my time, was when all the fairy godmothers in my group meet. It's kind of weird because we aren't all in the same time zone but everyone just says "Monday at seven." And somehow, no one ever seems to go looking for me in that time frame either. Some things about being a fairy godmother don't make sense.

There are a bunch of us there. Paula is one of them, of course, and there's Connie, the cat lady, and Granny, whose real name is Grace, but she's so stereotypically someone's granny that I have a hard time remembering her name. There's Brian, who reminds me of a football player. I think he's Italian but I'm not sure. And Sergei, who hardly speaks and is sort of ferrety-looking. I expect he's Ukrainian.

There's a tall, thin, black woman named Deliza with the most amazing braids. She almost never says anything, even less than Sergei, but she frequently nods her head. She usually sits in one of the most uncomfortable chairs but she's got such long legs that maybe it works for her.

There's two other guys who are almost as quiet, Jesus and Cole, who seem to prefer talking to each other than to us. They're both older, not quite as old as Grace, but like older adults and they spend most of their time whispering together, even though Jesus is broad and strong-looking and Cole looks like he can barely make himself stand up.

Sue keeps to herself even more than Deliza, and while she looks like she's pretty young, she acts older than dirt, like she might even be a senior—but given what Paula said, she's not and maybe not even the oldest here. Still, she makes me think of a female Yoda even if she isn't that wrinkled.

"We're back?" Paula asked when she saw me.

I nodded. "It looks like it worked," I said.

We started to talk a little about what happened, but Grace was listening and asked me to wait so we could all discuss it. So I was the start of the evening at the Fairy Godmother's meeting that Monday. I wasn't the only one who hadn't known about the Seniors—only about half of my group had heard of them.

They asked me about the training. Grace had learned a little, sort of as a by-product of being a grandmother and having her grandchildren always wishing for things. She'd learned to guard herself against accidently granting wishes that their parents wouldn't be happy about. But no one else had learned to meditate through the wishing requests.

"I think we should all pledge to start learning some sort

of meditation," Paula said. "It sounds like we could be more effective, and it will help prevent us from accidentally fulfilling bad wishes."

There were nods around. Not everyone looked excited, but even those that looked less than enthusiastic, like Sergei, appeared willing to do it. I mean, in the long run they all knew it would be a good thing. Sort of like how, in the long run, working up to running a marathon was good. It was just the practice that kind of sucked.

Paula was thrilled when I said I had granted a wish so that we wouldn't go back to that world. It was interesting that only Paula remembered the other world. Perhaps that was because I had contacted her there. Or maybe the other world hadn't touched anyone's lives enough for them to have noticed anything different? It was hard to say. But I was really thankful it was over.

And that Darren texted me the other night. But that's a whole different story.

About Bonnie Elizabeth

Bonnie Elizabeth has been writing since she was eight years old when she wrote her first book on several pieces of lined paper. The manuscript has long since been lost.

Since that time she has worked at a variety of jobs including veterinary receptionist, cemetery administrator and licensed acupuncturist. She has continued to write in a variety of venues, from blogging to writing about acupuncture under her full name and title, Bonnie Koenig, LAc.

Bonnie writes the popular Whisper series of novels as well as writing a variety of short fiction. You can find her books and stories at all your favorite ebook retailers.

Her website is BonnieElizabeth.com or find her on Facebook

Also by Bonnie Elizabeth

The Whisper Novels

Whisper Bound

Taken by the Sound

An Air of Suspicion

Little Dog Lost

Death Interrupted

Down in Whisper

A Haunting Whisper

A Haunting Attraction

Secrets Not Whispers

Whisper Short Stories

Ghost Case

Christmas Whispers

Radioactive Magic

Find them all at your favorite bookseller or check us out at
MyBigFatOrangeCat.com